All about My ...walkabouts

Ruskin Bond is known for his signature simplistic and witty writing style. He is the author of several bestselling short stories, novellas, collections, essays and children's books; and has contributed a number of poems and articles to various magazines and anthologies. At the age of twenty-three, he won the prestigious John Llewellyn Rhys Prize for his first novel, *The Room on the Roof*. He was also the recipient of the Padma Shri in 1999, Lifetime Achievement Award by the Delhi Government in 2012 and the Padma Bhushan in 2014.

Born in 1934, Ruskin Bond grew up in Jamnagar, Shimla, New Delhi and Dehradun. Apart from three years in the UK, he has spent all his life in India, and now lives in Landour, Mussoorie, with his adopted family.

RUSKIN BOND

All about My Walkabouts

RUPA

Published by
Rupa Publications India Pvt. Ltd 2021
7/16, Ansari Road, Daryaganj
New Delhi 110002

Sales centres:
Allahabad Bengaluru Chennai
Hyderabad Jaipur Kathmandu
Kolkata Mumbai

ISBN: 978-93-5520-060-0

Second impression 2022

10 9 8 7 6 5 4 3 2

Moral right of the author has been asserted.

Printed in India

CONTENTS

INTRODUCTION

Travelling is one of the most enriching experiences one can participate in. You don't need the best hotels, the most expensive means of travel or the top restaurants to experience the true essence of a place. The best way to get to know your destination, especially in India, is by sitting in roadside tea stalls, visiting tiny hole in the wall eateries that will serve you the most authentic flavours and by engaging in conversation with the local tour guide, not about the monument they're supposed to be taking you around, but about their family, how many generations have lived in the town, how the town has changed over the years and what are the hidden gems tucked away in the corners of the town.

In the last two years, people have been confined to their homes and haven't been able to venture out to travel, within their own countries or outside its boundaries. Since we cannot travel, the next best thing available to travellers and curious minds is books. Reading about new cultures, about people of various towns and cities opens readers up to a treasure trove of information and fascinating events, incidents and places.

This book offers its readers an insight into the various cities of India and the author's experiences in these cities and its people. The streets of Jaipur, the lesser-known paths available to trekkers, the Taj in Agra, the Dickensian streets of London and many more—this book has something to offer to every curious mind!

Ruskin Bond

ON THE HIGHWAY

For forty years I have been content living a life of modest excitements in Mussoorie. The world drives up here in season, for holidays and honeymoons, so I rarely feel the need to go down to the busy plains. But once or twice a year, in self-indulgent mood, or when my publishers prevail upon me, I give myself a 'treat', if you can call it that: a seven-hour drive to Delhi in a sturdy Ambassador taxi. Winter is the best time for such a visit. The hot winds of summer are best avoided, for once you have descended from the hills, the road becomes dusty, and in places something of an obstacle race.

I have known this highway over the years and I have seen it change imperceptibly. There wasn't much traffic on it in the 1940s, apart from the familiar bullock carts stacked high with sugarcane. The carts are still used, although the wooden wheels have given way to heavy tyres, and the bullocks to buffaloes. However, much of the sugarcane is now carried in trucks, and these 'kings of the road' have made it difficult for others to drive smoothly by day or safely by night. But I am told the trucks and the sugarcane keep the economy of the region going, so we shouldn't grumble too much.

I am told the same about all the cars and tourist buses that I complain about: what would happen to Uttaranchal's economy if they stopped coming! I quieten down then, but I wonder at the great speed at which they move. People come seeking nature and new experiences but have no interest in the world outside.

To me, the outside world is the reward of a highway journey. I like looking at the countryside, the passing scene, the people along the road (so it is just as well that I cannot drive). And even in the twenty-first century, when television channels claim to show us everything there is to see, it can be a revelation. Recently, on a trip to Delhi, we had to leave the main highway because of a disturbance near Meerut. Instead we had to drive through about a dozen villages in the sugarcane belt that dominates this area. It was a wonderful contrast, leaving the main road with its cafes, petrol pumps, factories and management institutes and entering the rural hinterland where very little had changed in a hundred years. Women with their faces veiled worked in the fields, old men smoked hookahs in their courtyards and a few children were playing guli-danda instead of cricket! It brought home to me the reality of India—urban life and rural life are still poles apart.

As I do not drive myself, I am the ideal person to have in the front seat; I repose complete confidence in the man behind the wheel. Sitting up front, I also see more of the road and the passing scene. Sardar Manmohan Singh shares this interest, but he has a far sharper eye. Manmohan is one of Mussoorie's better taxi drivers. He is also a keen wildlife enthusiast. It always amazes me how he is able to drive through the Siwaliks, on a winding hill road, and still be able to keep his eye open for denizens of the surrounding forest.

'See that cheetal!' he will exclaim, or 'What a fine sambhar!' or 'Just look at that elephant!'

All this at high speed. And before I've had time to get more than a fleeting glimpse of one of these creatures, we are well past them.

Manmohan swears that he has seen a tiger crossing the road near the Mohand Pass, and as he is a person of some integrity, I have to believe him. I think the tiger appears especially for Manmohan.

Another wildlife enthusiast is my bank manager and old friend Vishal Ohri, with whom I have been on some memorable drives. Unlike our car drivers, he is in no hurry to reach our destination and will stop every now and then, in order to examine the footprints of an elephant or a leopard. He also takes great pleasure in pointing out large dollops of fresh elephant dung, proof that wild elephants are in the vicinity. The prospect of being charged by an angry elephant has never worried him, and he holds forth at great length on the benefits of elephant dung— how it can be used to reinforce mud walls, for instance—till I urge him to get a move on before nightfall.

On one occasion, Vishal decided to give me a treat by taking a short cut from Hardwar through the Rajaji Sanctuary and out at the Mohand Pass. Vishal enjoys his driving, especially in rough conditions; unfortunately, his ancient Fiat was in poor condition, and halfway through the sanctuary, while we were crossing a boulder-strewn *rao* (a semi-dry riverbed) the door on my side fell off and I very nearly went with it. For the rest of the journey, I had an uninterrupted view of the wildlife in the sanctuary—two peahens, a startled porcupine and a herd of tame buffaloes.

◆

Driving by night is not always so risible. Most accidents on the main highway road occur in the early hours when drivers fall asleep at the wheel: their vehicles overturn, or run into trees and ditches, or collide with other vehicles. Before dawn breaks, the road has taken its toll of several lives.

It was late Christmas Eve in the 1970s, when my thirty-year-old half-brother Harold set out from Dehra in his father's car, to try and get to Delhi in time for a party at the Anglo-Indian Club. Although he was a good driver, having taken part in car rallies and other tests of speed and endurance, he had become a heavy drinker and he was in no condition to undertake a long and arduous drive late at night. He was alone, and as he was killed instantly (or so we were told), we never knew all the circumstances of his death. Apparently his car had been caught and crushed between two trucks, which had speedily disappeared into the night.

Harold was always a bit of a tearaway. He was attractive to women, but they had a hard time looking after him. And he wrecked their lives in addition to his own. There were lessons about life and highways that he never learnt.

But perhaps there aren't any lessons to be learnt. A few months after Harold, my second half-brother was killed in a motorcycle accident. He was the careful one, who seldom took risks. He was sober that night, as on all others, and mindful of rules, but someone else on the road was not.

THE GRAND TRUNK ROAD

There is a fantasy journey that I have always wanted to make, but one that I know I never will: the long, long journey along the Grand Trunk Road from Calcutta to Peshawar.

For the Grand Trunk Road is a river. It may not be as sacred as the Ganga, which it greets at Kanpur and Varanasi, but it is just as permanent. It's a river of life, an unending stream of humanity intent on reaching their destination and getting there most of the time.

A long day's journey into night, that's how I would describe the saga of the truck driver, that knight errant, or rather errant knight, of India's Via Appia. Undervalued, underpaid and often disparaged, he drives all day and sometimes all night, carrying the country's goods and produce for hundreds of miles on the GT Road, across state borders, through lawless tracts, at all seasons and in all weathers. We blame him for hogging the middle of the road, but he is usually overloaded and if he veers too much to the left or right he is quite likely to topple over, burying himself and crew under bricks or gas cylinders, sugarcane or

TV sets. More than the railwayman, the truck driver is modern India's lifeline, and yet his life is held cheap. He drinks, he swears, occasionally he picks up HIV, and frequently he is killed or badly injured. But we cannot do without him.

In the old, old days, when Muhammad Tughlaq, Sultan of Delhi, streamlined the country's roads, bullock carts and camel caravans were the chief transporters. In 1333, when the Moroccan traveller Ibn Battuta visited India, he was deeply impressed by the Sultan's road network. Sher Shah Suri, who ruled from 1540 till 1545, made further improvements, especially to the GT Road. He built caravanserais and inns for travellers, and planted fine trees along the GT Road and other important highways. Horsemen, carts and palanquin bearers jostled for pride of position, much as our motorists do today. Traffic was slow-moving, and the best way to get ahead was to mount a horse and canter from stage to stage, that is, between twelve and fifteen miles a day.

Invading armies had, of course, made use of the Road long before the British gained control of northern India. On this same stretch of the highway, the Persian invader Nadir Shah defeated the Mughal Emperor in 1739. In a battle lasting two hours, over 20,000 of the Emperor's soldiers were killed. The next day Nadir Shah marched to Delhi, to sack the city and massacre its inhabitants. The treasure harvest of Delhi was fair game for acquisitive kings and warlords.

When the British consolidated their power in India, they found the Road, stretching as it did from Calcutta to Peshawar, a great line of communication. Kipling's 'regiment a-marchin' down the GT Road' was a common enough sight throughout the nineteenth century. During the 1857 uprising, after the British were ousted from Delhi, their army assembled at Ambala and came marching down the GT Road to lay siege to the city of Delhi. A few years later, a junior officer, recalling the march, wrote:

> The stars were bright in the dark deep sky and the fireflies flashed from bush to bush... Along the road came the heavy roll of the guns, mixed with the jangling of bits and the clanking of the scabbards of the cavalry. The infantry marched behind with a deep, dull tread. Camels and bullock carts, with innumerable camp servants, toiled away for miles in the rear, while gigantic elephants, pulling the heavy guns, came lumbering down the road.

Some thirty years after the 1857 uprising came the Afghan Wars, and the GT Road became an all-important route for the British army proceeding towards Peshawar and the Khyber Pass. Those were the days of military manoeuvres all over north India, and my grandfather, a foot-soldier in the mould of Kipling's 'soldiers three', found himself 'route marching', that is, foot-slogging all over northern and central India. Wives and children followed the regiment wherever it was sent, and military camps and cantonments sprang up everywhere. Children were often born in the course of these marches and troop movements: my father at Shahjahanpur (not far from the Road), his brothers and sisters at places as far apart as Barrackpore, Campbellpur and Dera Ismail Khan!

The tedium of the march was broken only by the sight of fields of golden corn stretching towards the horizon, with mango groves rising like islands from the flat plain; but for the most part it was monotonous tramping, exemplified in this marching song of Kipling's:

Oh, there's them Indian temples to admire when you see,
There's the peacock round the corner
An' the monkey up the tree.
With our best foot first
And the Road a-sliding past,
An every bloomin' camping-ground
Exactly like the last.

Kipling immortalized the Road in *Kim* and *Barrack-Room Ballads* (he had a strong empathy with the common soldier), and but for him, few outside of India would have heard of the Grand Trunk Road. But Kipling would not recognize the Road today. Cars, buses, tractors, trucks, all thunder down the highway, and even the bullock carts are equipped with heavy tyres. It's a very democratic mix. Nowhere else in the world are you likely to find such a variety of traffic, or so many impediments to vehicular progress—cows, cart-horses, buffaloes, cyclists, stray hens, stray villagers, stray policemen.

'Proceed at your own risk.' You could call this the motto of the Road, a motto vividly illustrated by overturned lorries lying in ditches, buses upended against trees or dangling over culverts, fancy cars crushed into concertina shapes, squashed cats and dogs, mangled drivers and passengers. These are common sights, along with the endless panorama of field, factory, village or township.

For the towns and cities grow bigger by the day. They spread octopus-like over the rural landscape, and the traffic spills out in an endless, honking procession of humankind on wheels. 'OK Tata', proclaims the truck in front of you, and it would be wise to keep your distance. What's your choice of vehicle for making progress on the Road? Motorcycle, taxi, limousine, or buffalo cart? Mine's a steamroller. No one pushes it around.

◆

I have never travelled the entire length of the Road, but I have driven along stretches of it. The most memorable one was with Gurbachan Singh.

As his taxi weaved its way in and out of the Amritsar traffic, and headed for Delhi, Gurbachan Singh took his hand off the horn and gave me a brief triumphant look.

'What do you think of my horn?' he asked.

'Oh, it's a fine horn,' I said, wringing out my ears. 'It couldn't be louder.'

'You can hear it half a mile ahead,' said Gurbachan proudly, as he blasted off at two young men who were sharing a bicycle. They moved out of the way with alacrity.

'It makes a lot of noise in the car, too,' I said, and added hastily, 'not that I object, you know…'

'Doesn't your horn have more than one tone of voice?' asked a fellow traveller with a trace of irritation.

'Two!' claimed Gurbachan. 'Male and female. Just see!' And he produced a high note and then a low note on the horn, both equally ear-shattering. Ahead of us, a tonga ran off the road and on to the cart track.

'This is one terrific horn,' said Gurbachan. I have had it made especially for this taxi. No foreign horns for me. They are not loud enough. Indian horns are best.'

'Indian noise is best,' said the fellow traveller.

In an interval of comparative quiet, I found myself reflecting on the nature of sound—the unpleasantness of some sounds, and the sweetness of others, and why certain sounds (like motor horns) can be sweet to some and hideous to others. The sweetest sound of all, I decided, was silence. There are many kinds of silence—the silence of an empty room, the silence of the mountains, the silence of prayer or the enforced silence of loneliness—but the best kind of silence, I concluded, was the silence that comes after the cessation of noise.

'It was made in the Jama Masjid area,' continued Gurbachan, interrupting my thoughts. 'Seventy-five rupees only. Made by hand, to my own specification. There's only one drawback: it must not get wet!'

As his hand settled down on the horn again, I thought of praying for rain, but the sky being clear and blue, I decided that a prayer would be an unreasonable demand on the Creator.

'Ah, but you don't know what it is to have a horn like this one. Try it, sir. Why don't you try it for yourself?'

'Oh, that's all right,' I assured him. 'You have proved its excellence already.'

'No, you must try it. I insist that you try it!' He was like a big boy, suddenly generous, determined on sharing a new toy with a younger brother.

He grabbed my hand and placed it on the horn, and, as I felt it give a little, a thrill of pleasure rushed up my arm. I pressed hard, and a stream of music flowed in and out of the car. Now I could understand the happiness and the supreme self-confidence of Gurbachan and all drivers like him; for, with a horn like his, one felt the power and glory that belongs to the kings of the Road.

For the rest of the journey Gurbachan drove and I blew the horn.

The fellow passenger, no doubt realizing that he was locked into a taxi with two lunatics, was too terrified to say a word.

RUNNING AWAY

Once, during my schooldays, my friend Daljit and I decided to run away. The main reason for running away was not to get back to the bazaars of Dehra, which we both missed, but to reach my uncle's ship in Jamnagar, Gujarat.

Uncle Jim was one of my father's cousins. He used to write to me off and on throughout the years. His letters came in envelopes that bore colourful stamps of different countries. They came from Valparaiso, San Diego, San Francisco, Buenos Aires, Dar-es-Salaam, Mombasa, Freetown, Singapore, Bombay, Marseilles, London...these were some of the places where Uncle Jim's ship called. He was seldom on the same route, and seemed to move leisurely across the oceans of the earth, calling at ports which had only the most romantic associations for me, for I had already read Stevenson, Captain Marryat, some Conrad and W.W. Jacobs.

In his letters, Uncle Jim often spoke of my joining him at sea—'When you are a little older, Ruskin.'

But I felt I was old enough then. I was sick of school and

sick of my guardian. But that was not all. I was in love with the world. I wanted to see the world, every corner of it, the places I had read about in books—the junks and sampans of Hong Kong, the palm-fringed lagoons of the Indies, the streets of London, the beautiful ebony-skinned people of Africa, the bright birds and exotic plants of the Amazon...

When Uncle Jim's last letter had arrived, telling me that his ship would call at Jamnagar towards the end of the month, I felt a deep thrill of anticipation. Here was my chance at last! True, Uncle Jim had said nothing about my joining him, but he was not to know that I was seriously considering it.

It was not simply a question of walking out of school and taking a quick ride down to the docks. Jamnagar, on the west coast, was at least eight hundred miles from my school. I doubt if I would have made the attempt if Daljit had not agreed to come too. It isn't much fun running away on your own. It is even worse if you have a companion who is full of enthusiasm at the beginning and then backs out at the last moment. This leaves one feeling defeated and crushed. Daljit was not that kind of companion. He meant the things he said. About a month earlier, when I had told him of my uncle's ship and my wish to get to it, he had said, without a moment's hesitation: 'I'm coming too!' Daljit lived impulsively. Sometimes he made mistakes. But he never went halfway and stopped. Someone had to stop him; otherwise he did whatever it was he set out to do.

Running away from school! It is not to be recommended to everyone. Parents and teachers would disapprove. Or would they, deep down in their hearts? Everyone has wanted to run away, at some time in his life: if not from a bad school or an unhappy home, then from something equally unpleasant. Running away seems to be in the best of traditions. Huck

Finn did it. So did Master Copperfield and Oliver Twist. So did Kim. Various enterprising young men have run away to sea. Most great men have run away from school at some stage in their lives; and if they haven't, then perhaps it is something they should have done.

Anyway, Daljit and I ran away from school, and we did it quite successfully too, up to a point. But then, all this happened in India, which, though it forms only two per cent of the world's land mass, has 15 per cent of its population, and so it is an easy place to hide in, or be lost in, or disappear in, and never be seen or heard of again!

Not that we intended to disappear. We were headed for a particular place, and as soon as I took my first step into the unknown, that first step on the slippery pine needles below the school, I knew quite definitely that I wasn't running away from anything, but that I was running *towards* something. Call it a dream, if you like. I was running towards a dream.

A narrow path ran downhill from the school to the road to Dehra, and we followed it until it levelled out, running parallel with the small stream that rumbled down the mountainside. We followed the stream for a mile, walking swiftly and silently, until we met the bridle-path which was little more than a mule-track going steeply down the last hills to the valley.

The going was easy. We knew the road well. And by the time we reached the last foothills it was beginning to rain, not heavily, but as a light, thin drizzle.

We took shelter in a small dhaba on the outskirts of a village. The dhabawallah was sleeping, and his dog, a mangy pariah with only one ear, sniffed at us in a friendly way instead of chasing us off the premises. We sat down on an old bench and watched the sun rising over the distant mountains.

This is something I have always remembered. Not because it was a more beautiful sunrise than on any other day, but because the special importance of that morning made me look at everything in a new way, hence the details still stand out in my memory.

As the sky grew lighter, the pines and deodars stood out clearly, and the birds came to life. A black-bird started it all with a low, mellow call, and then the thrushes began chattering in the bushes. A barbet shrieked monotonously at the top of a spruce tree, and, as the sky grew lighter still, a flock of bright green parrots flew low over the trees.

The drizzle continued and there was a bright crimson glow in the east. And then, quite, suddenly, the sun shot through a gap in the clouds, and the lush green monsoon grass sprang into relief. Both Daljit and I were wonderstruck. Never before had we been up so early. Hundreds of spiderwebs, which were spun in trees and bushes and on the grass, where they would not normally have been noticed, were now clearly visible, spangled with gold and silver raindrops. The strong silk threads of the webs held the light rain and the sun, making each drop of water look like a tiny jewel.

A great wild dahlia, its scarlet flowers drenched and heavy, sprawled over the hillside and an emerald-green grasshopper reclined on a petal, stretching its legs in the sunshine.

The dhabawallah was now up. His dog, emboldened by his master's presence, began to bark at us. The man lit a charcoal fire in a choolah, and put on it a kettle of water to boil.

'Would you like to eat something?' he asked conversationally in Hindi.

'No, just tea for us,' I said.

He placed two brass tumblers on a table.

'The milk hasn't yet been delivered,' he said. 'You're very early.'

'We'll take the tea without milk,' said Daljit. 'But give us lots of sugar.'

'Sugar is costly these days. But because you are schoolboys, and need more, you can help yourselves.'

'Oh, we are not schoolboys,' I said hurriedly.

'Not at all,' added Daljit.

'We are just tourists,' I lied unconvincingly.

'We have to catch the early train at Dehra,' offered Daljit.

'But there's no train before ten o'clock,' said the puzzled dhabawallah.

'It is the ten o'clock train we are catching!' said Daljit smartly. 'Do you think we will be down in time?'

'Oh yes, there's plenty of time…'

The dhabawallah poured out steaming hot tea into the tumblers and placed the sugar bowl in front of us. 'At first I thought you were schoolboys,' he said with a laugh. 'I thought you were running away.'

Daljit almost gave us away by laughing nervously.

'What made you think that?' he asked.

'Oh, I've been here many years,' the dhabawallah replied, gesturing towards the small clearing in which his little wooden stall stood, almost like a trading outpost in a wild country. 'Schoolboys always pass this way when they're running away!'

'Do many run away?' I asked. I felt a little downcast at the thought that Daljit and I were not the first to embark on such an adventure.

'Not many. Just two or three every year. They get as far as the railway station in Dehra and there they're caught!'

'It is silly of them to get caught,' said Daljit disgustedly.

'Are they always caught?' I asked.

'Always! I give them a glass of tea on their way down, and I give them a glass of tea on their way up, when they are returning with their teachers.'

'Well, you won't be seeing *us* again,' said Daljit, ignoring the warning look that I gave him.

'Ah, but you aren't schoolboys!' said the shopkeeper, beaming at us. 'And you aren't running away!'

We paid for our tea and hurried on down the path. The parrots flew over again, screeching loudly, and settled in a lichee tree. The sun was warmer now, and, as the altitude decreased, the temperature and humidity rose and we could almost smell the heat of the plains rising to meet us.

The hills levelled out into the rolling countryside, patterned with fields. Rice had been planted out, and the sugarcane was waist-high.

The path had become quite slushy. Removing our shoes and wrapping them in newspaper, we walked barefoot in the soft mud. All these little out-of-routine acts simply added to our excitement and thrill, making everything quite unforgettable for life.

'It's about three miles into Dehra,' I said. 'We must go round the town. By now, everyone in school will be up and they'll have found out we've gone!'

'We must avoid the Dehra station then,' said Daljit.

'We'll walk to the next station, Raiwala. Then we'll hop onto the first train that comes along.'

'How far must we walk?'

'About ten miles.'

'Ten miles!' Daljit looked dismayed. 'It'll take us all day!'

'Well, we can't stop here nor can we wander about in Dehra,

neither can we enter the station. We have to keep on walking.'

'All right. We'll keep on walking. I suppose the beginning of an adventure is always the most difficult part.'

Soon, the fields were giving way to jungle. But there were still some fields of sugarcane stretching away from the railway lines.

'How much further do we have to walk?' asked Daljit impatiently. 'Is Raiwala in the middle of the jungle?'

'Yes, I think it is. We've covered about four miles I suppose. Six to go! It's funny how some miles seem longer than others. It depends on what one is thinking about, I suppose. If our thoughts are pleasant, the miles are not so long.'

'Then let's keep thinking pleasant thoughts. Isn't there a short cut anywhere? You've been in these forests before.'

'We'll take the fire-path through the jungle. It'll save us three or four miles. But we'll have to swim or wade across a small river. The rains have only just started, so the water shouldn't be too swift or deep.'

Heavy forests have paths cut through them at various places to prevent forest fires from spreading easily. These paths are not used much by people since they don't lead anywhere in particular, but they are frequently used by the larger animals.

We had gone about a mile along the path when we heard the sound of rushing water. The path emerged from the forest of sal trees and stopped on the banks of the small river I had mentioned earlier. The main bridge across the river stood on the main road, about three miles downstream.

'It isn't more than waist-deep anywhere,' I said. 'But the water is swift and the stones are slippery.'

We removed our clothes and tied everything into two bundles which we carried on our heads. Daljit was a well-built boy, strong in the arms and thighs. I was slimmer. But I had quick reflexes.

The stones were quite slippery underfoot, and we stumbled, hindering rather than helping each other. We stopped in midstream, waist-deep, hesitating about going any further for fear of being swept off our feet.

'I can hardly stand,' said Daljit.

'It shouldn't get worse,' I said hopefully. But the current was strong, and I felt very wobbly at the knees.

Daljit tried to move forward, but slipped and went over backwards into the water, bringing me down too. He began kicking and thrashing about in fear, but eventually, using me as a support, he came up spouting water like a whale.

When we found we were not being swept away, we stopped struggling and cautiously made our way to the opposite bank, but we had been thrust about twenty yards downstream.

We rested on warm sand, while a hot sun beat down on us. Daljit sucked at a cut in his hand. But we were soon up and walking again, hungry now, and munching biscuits.

'We haven't far to go,' I said.

'I don't want to think about it,' said Daljit.

We shuffled along the forest path, tired but not discouraged.

Soon we were on the main road again, and there were fields and villages on either side. A cool breeze came across the open plain, blowing down from the hills. In the fields there was a gentle swaying movement as the wind stirred the sugarcane. Then the breeze came down the road, and dust began to swirl and eddy around us. Out of the dust, behind us, came the rumble of cart wheels.

'Ho! Heeyah! Heeyah!' shouted the driver of the cart. The bullocks snorted and came lumbering through the dust. We moved to the side of the road.

'Are you going to Raiwala?' called Daljit. 'Can you take

us with you?'

'Climb up!' said the man, and we ran through the dust and clambered on to the back of the moving cart.

The cart lurched forward and rattled and bumped so much that we had to cling to its sides to avoid falling off. It smelt of grass and mint and cow-dung cakes. The driver had a red cloth tied round his head, and wore a tight vest and a dhoti. He was smoking a beedi and yelling at his bullocks, and he seemed to have forgotten our presence. We were too busy clinging to the sides of the cart to bother about making conversation. Before long we were involved in the traffic of Raiwala—a small but busy market town. We jumped off the bullock cart and walked beside it.

'Should we offer him any money?' I asked.

'No. He will be offended. He is not a taxi driver.'

'All right, we'll just say thank you.'

We called out our thanks to the cart driver, but he didn't look back. He appeared to be talking to his bullocks.

'I'm hungry,' declared Daljit. 'We haven't had a proper meal since last night.'

'Then let's eat,' I said. 'Come on, Daljit.'

We walked through the small Raiwala bazaar, looking in at the tea and sweet shops until we found the cheapest-looking dhaba. A servant-boy brought us rice and dal and Daljit ordered an ounce of ghee which he poured over the curry. The meal cost us two rupees but we could have as much dal as we wanted, and between us we finished four bowls of it.

'We'll rest at the station,' I said, as we emerged from the dhaba. 'We'll buy second-class tickets, and rest in the first-class waiting room. No one will check on us. We look first class, don't we?'

'Not after that walk through the jungle,' replied Daljit.

But we did occupy the best waiting room and Daljit made himself comfortable in an armchair. A train eventually came chugging in, and we were soon on our way to Delhi.

It didn't take us long to find a hotel once we got off at the Old Delhi Railway Station. It was called the Great Oriental Hotel, and was just behind the police station in Chandni Chowk. It didn't pretend to be even a third-class hotel, and for five rupees we were given a small back room which had a window overlooking the godown of an Afghan spice merchant. The powerful smell of asafoetida came up from the courtyard below.

We were tired and hot, so we tossed our belongings down on the floor and took turns at the bathroom tap. Then we stretched out on the only cot in the room and slept through the afternoon, oblivious to the noises from the street, the attentions of the insect population in the hotel mattress, and the creaking of the old fan overhead.

It was late evening when we woke up, and we were hungry again. Daljit opened the door and shouted. Presently a servant-boy appeared.

'Bring us tea, toast, two big omelettes, and a bottle of tomato sauce,' ordered Daljit with a confidence that I wished I had.

The omelettes, when they arrived twenty minutes later, were tiny. Both had obviously been made from one egg. The sauce had been diluted with water, and the toasts were burnt. The salt was damp, and we had to prise open the salt-cellar to get to it. The pepper, however, came out in a generous rush and made up the major portion of the meal. As our hunger had not been satisfied by this poor fare, we ordered eggs again, boiled eggs this time. No matter how tiny, they would have to be whole.

'Let's go out,' said Daljit after we had eaten the eggs. 'It's stuffy in here.'

'I'm still sleepy,' I said.

'Then I'll go out for a little while. I may go to the gurdwara.'

'All right, but don't get lost.'

Drowsy, I closed my eyes, but the sounds of the city's unceasing traffic came through the window. Ships and distant ports seemed very far away but so did hills and mountain streams.

I fell asleep and woke up only when Daljit returned.

'I've solved our problem!' he said, beaming. 'We won't bother with the train. I met a truck driver, and he has offered to take us as far as Jaipur. That's more than a hundred miles. It will be quite safe to take a train from Jaipur.'

'When can your friend take us?'

'The truck leaves at four o'clock in the morning.'

'There's no rest for the wicked,' I said. 'Still, the less time we lose the better. It's Wednesday, and my uncle's ship might sail on Saturday. What will we have to pay?'

'Nothing. It's a free ride. The driver is a Sikh, and I persuaded him that we are related to each other through the marriage of my brother-in-law to his sister-in-law's niece!'

◆

At four the next morning we made our way towards the Red Fort, its ramparts dark against the starry sky. The streets which had been teeming with so much life the previous evening were now deserted. The street lamps shed lonely pools of light on the pavements. The occasional car glided silently past, but it belonged to another kind of world altogether.

Near the Fort we found a couple of dhabas which were still open. They did business with the truck drivers who slept by day and drove by night.

Our driver, a tall, bearded Sikh, loomed over us out of the

darkness. He had a companion with him, also a Sikh, who was still in his underwear.

'You can get in at the back,' said the driver in his thick Punjabi which I could follow sufficiently well. 'We'll be off in a few minutes.'

The truck was parked beneath a peepul tree. We pulled ourselves up into the back of the open truck, only to find our way barred by what seemed at first to be a prehistoric monster.

The monster snorted once, stamped heavily on the boards, and sent us tumbling backwards.

'Bhaiyyaji!' cried Daljit to the driver. There's some kind of animal in here!'

'Don't worry, it's only Mumta,' said our friend.

'But what is it doing in here?'

'She is going with us. I am taking her to the market in Jaipur. So get in with her boys, and make yourselves comfortable.'

There was now enough light to enable us to take a closer look at our travelling companion. She was a full-grown buffalo from the Punjab.

'An excellent buffalo,' said Daljit, who appeared to be familiar with the finer points of these animals. 'Notice her blue eyes!'

'I didn't know buffaloes had blue eyes,' I said dryly.

'Only the best buffaloes have them,' said Daljit. 'Blue-eyed buffaloes give more milk than brown-eyed ones.'

Fortunately for us, the Sardarji started the truck and an early morning breeze, blowing across the river, swept away some of the stench so typical of buffaloes.

We were soon out of Delhi and bowling along at a fair speed on the road to Jaipur. The recent rain had waterlogged low-lying areas, and the herons, cranes and snipe were numerous. Fields and trees were alive with strange, beautiful birds: the long-tailed king crow, blue jays and weaver birds, and occasionally the great white-headed kite, which is said to be Garuda, Lord Vishnu's famous steed.

As we travelled further into Rajasthan, the peacocks became more numerous; so did the camels loping along the side of the road in straight, orderly lines. And, as the vegetation grew less and the desert took over, the people themselves grew more colourful, as though to make up for the absence of colour in the landscape. The women wore wide red skirts, and gold and silver ornaments. They were handsome, tall, fair and strong. The men were tall too and the older among them had flowing white beards.

As the day grew older, and the sun rose higher in the sky, the traffic on the road increased; but our truck driver, instead of slowing down, drove faster. Perhaps he was in a hurry to dispose of the buffalo. Soon he was trying to overtake another truck.

The truck in front was moving fast too, and its driver had no intention of giving up the middle of the road. It was piled high with stacks of sugarcane.

'It's going to be a race!' cried Daljit excitedly, standing up against the buffalo, in order to get a better view.

The road was not wide enough to take two large vehicles at once, and as the other truck wouldn't make way, ours had to fall in behind it, almost suffocating us with the exhaust fumes. We were thrown to the floorboards as the truck lurched over the ruts in the rough road, and Mumta, getting nervous, almost trampled upon us. Then there was a tremendous bump, a grinding of brakes, and we came to a stop.

As the dust cleared, we made out our driver's bearded face gazing anxiously down at us.

'Are you all right?' he asked gruffly.

'I think so,' I said.

'Did you overtake the other truck?' asked Daljit.

'No,' grunted our friend. 'He would not give way. You had better come in front.'

We agreed without any hesitation and his assistant rather grudgingly joined the buffalo.

After a few miles, the driver became friendly and told us that his name was Gurnam Singh.

It was getting dark by the time we reached Jaipur, so we were not able to see much of the city. We spent the night in the truck, sleeping in the back with Gurnam Singh. Mumta had been disposed of on the way. Jaipur nights can be chilly, even in summer, so Gurnam Singh considerately shared his bedding with us. Because he was accustomed to sleeping in the body of the truck, he was soon asleep, snoring loudly and rhythmically. Daljit and I tossed and turned restlessly. He kicked me several times in the night. The floor of the truck was hard, and retained various buffalo smells.

We had hardly fallen asleep (or so it seemed), when Gurnam Singh woke us up, saying that it was almost four o'clock and that he had to start on his return journey, this time with a load of red sandstone.

'What a life!' exclaimed Daljit, sleepily rubbing his eyes with one hand. 'I'd hate to be a truck driver.'

'One has to live somehow,' philosophized Gurnam Singh. 'I like driving. I knew how to drive when I was merely six or seven. The money is not so bad, either. Now, when I get back to Delhi, I will have two days off, which I will spend with my wife and children. Goodbye friends, and if you pass through Delhi again, you will find me near the walls of the Red Fort.'

We waved to him as he shot off in his truck, throwing up

huge clouds of dust, making a great noise and probably waking the local inhabitants. Dogs barked, and a cock began to crow.

We were on the outskirts of the city, facing a large lake. On the other side was open country, bare hills and desert. We could also make out the ruins of a building—probably a palace or a hunting lodge—among some thorn bushes and babul trees.

'Let's go out there,' suggested Daljit. 'We can bathe in the lake and rest. Then later in the morning we can come into the city and find out about trains.'

We set out along the shores of the lake, and it was a good half-hour before we reached the opposite bank.

There was no one in the fields, but a camel was going round and round a well, drawing up water in small trays. Smoke rose from houses in a nearby village, and the notes of a flute floated over to us on the still morning air.

It took us about twenty minutes to reach the ruin, which seemed like an old hunting lodge put up by some Rajput prince when game must have been plentiful.

The gate of the lodge was blocked with rubble, but part of the wall had crumbled apart and we climbed through the gap and found ourselves in a stone-paved courtyard in the centre of which stood a dry, disused stone fountain. A small peepul tree was growing from the crack in the floor of the fountain. Finding nothing to do there, we made our way to the railway tracks again.

Daljit and I snuck on to a goods train. It was a hard night's journey. The train was agonizingly slow and stopped at many places. At one small station, a number of sacks filled with what must have been cattle-fodder were tossed into the wagon, almost burying us in our fitful sleep. But we found they were comfortable to rest on and lay stretched out on top of them until the first light of morning.

As the sky cleared, we knew we were not far from our journey's end. The landscape had undergone a complete change. We had left the desert for the coastal plain.

The tall waving palms parted, and then I spotted the sea.

It was the sea as I had always dreamt of it ever since my days in Kathiawar with my father. It was vast, lonely and blue, blue as the sky was blue, and the first ship I saw was a sailing-ship, an Arab dhow, listing slightly in the mild breeze that blew onto the shore.

The train stopped at a small bridge spanning a stream which wound its way across the plain down to the sea. We got down there and trudged the rest of the way to our destination.

Two hours later we were at Jamnagar.

We stopped near a small tea shop and watched other people eating laddoos and bhelpuri. We couldn't even afford a coconut.

'Where is the harbour?' I asked the shopkeeper.

'Two miles from here,' he replied.

'Are there any ships in the port?' I asked, relieved yet anxious.

'What do you want with a ship?'

'What does anyone want with a ship?'

'Well there's only one and it sails today, so you had better hurry if you want to go away on it.'

'Let's go,' said Daljit.

'Wait!' said a young man who was lounging against the counter. 'It will take you almost an hour to get there if you walk. I will take you in my cart.' He pointed to a shabby pony cart close by. The pony did not look as though it wanted to go anywhere.

'My pony is fast!' said the young man, following our glances. 'Never go by appearances. She may look tired but she runs like a champion! Get in friends, I will charge you only one rupee.'

'We don't have any money,' I said. 'We'll walk.'

'Fifty paisa, then,' he said. 'Fifty paisa and a glass of tea. Jump in my friends!'

'All right,' agreed Daljit. 'There's no time to lose. Fifty paisa and buy your own tea.'

We climbed into the cart, and the youth jumped up in front and cracked his whip. The pony lurched forward, the wheels rattled and shook, and we set off down the bazaar road at a tremendous trot.

'I didn't know you had fifty paisa left,' I said.

'I don't,' Daljit replied. 'But we'll worry about that later. Your uncle can pay!'

As soon as we were out of the town and on the open road to the sea, the pony went faster. She couldn't help doing so, as the road was downhill. The wind blew my hair across my eyes, and the salty tang of the sea was in the air.

Daljit shook me in his excitement.

'We will soon be at the harbour,' he yelled joyfully. 'And then away at last!'

The driver called out endearments to his pony, and, exhilarated by the sea breeze and the comparative speed of his carriage, he burst into song. As we turned a bend in the road, the sea-front came into view. There were several small dhows close to the shore, and fishing-boats were beached on the sand. The fishermen were drying their nets while their children ran naked in the surf. A steamer stood out on the sea and though I could not make out its name from that distance, I was sure it was the *Iris*.

The cart stopped at the beginning of the pier, and we tumbled out and began running along the pier. But even as we ran, it became clear to me that the ship was moving away from us, moving out to the sea. Its propeller sent small waves rippling back to the pier.

'Captain!' I shouted. 'Uncle Jim! Wait for us!'

A lascar standing in the stern waved to us; but that was all. I stood at the end of the pier, waving my hands and shouting into the wind.

'Captain! Uncle Jim! Wait for us!'

Nobody answered. The seagulls, wheeling in the wake of the steamer, seemed to take up the cry—'Captain, Captain...'

The ship drew further away, gaining speed. And still I called to it in a hoarse, pleading voice. Yokohama, San Diego, Valparaiso, London, all slipped away for ever...

BEER AT CHHUTMALPUR AND OTHER SMALL-TOWN CHARMS

On the way back from Delhi, just outside the small market-town of Chhutmalpur, I am greeted by a large signboard above a small shop with just two words on it: COLD BEER. After a gruelling five-hour drive in the heat and dust of summer, a glass of chilled beer is welcome, so I ask the driver to stop. Otherwise I would have no reason to break my journey here.

Chhutmalpur is not the sort of place you would choose to retire in. It was last in the news when a young Dalit couple was burnt alive by their disapproving families. Only its Sunday market gives it some charm, when the varied produce of the rural interior finds its way on to the dusty pavements and the air is rich with noise, colour and odours. There are carpets of red chillies and stacks of grain, vegetables and seasonal fruits; bangles of lac and wooden artifacts; colourful underwear; cheap toys for the children; sweets of every description and churan to go with them. ('*Lakar hajam, patther hajam*' cries the churan-seller. Digest wood, digest stones. When I tried the digestive pill, it appeared to be one part asafoetida and one part gunpowder.) Apart from this, Chhutmalpur has little to recommend it.

Which could also be said about Najibabad, where I stopped some forty years ago while on my way to Pauri-Garhwal. I was accompanying a friend to his village above the Nayar river. Getting there involved taking a train from Dehra Dun upto Luxor (across the Ganga), hopping on to another train, then getting off again at Najibabad and waiting for a bus to take us through the Tarai to Kotdwar, a little town in the foothills that seemed to lack any kind of character.

Najibabad must have been one of the least inspiring places on earth. Hot, dusty, apparently lifeless. We spent two hours at the bus stand—waiting for the bus driver who had gone missing—in the company of several donkeys, also quartered there. We were told that the area had once been the favourite hunting ground of a notorious dacoit, Sultana Daku, whose fortress overlooked the barren plain. I could understand him taking up dacoity— what else was there to do in such a place?—and presumed that he looked elsewhere for his loot, for in Najibabad there was nothing worth taking. In due course he was betrayed and was hanged by the British, when they should instead have given him an OBE for stirring up the sleepy countryside.

It was close to noon before the missing bus driver turned up, a little worse for some late-night drinking. I could sympathize with him. If in 1940 Najibabad drove you to dacoity, in 1960 it drove you to drink.

Chhutmalpur and Najibabad are not unique. The genuine small town of the great plains is still a desperate place. The following lines I wrote about a town I visited briefly in the late 1950s could apply to any small town in UP or Bihar or Bengal:

Every mohalla was congested and insanitary, and all the roads narrow and dusty...Near the masjid, I saw a gang of boys chase a terrified bow-legged dwarf. Two emaciated cows, that probably could no longer provide milk, roamed about in a state of semi-starvation. A group of eunuchs dressed in cheap silk ghagras strolled barefoot down the road, their long, gaunt faces made up with rouge and kajal. The jeering boys forgot about the dwarf and turned on them.

Through my long walk I was followed by a small, distracted goat. She stayed with me till I found a tonga, drawn by a lean, listless mare and driven by an ancient Muslim with a yellowing beard...

At the bus stop there was confusion. Newly arrived passengers, looking sleepy and dishevelled, were surrounded on all sides by a sea of mud and rain water, while scores of tongas and cycle rickshaws jostled each other in trying to cater to them. As a result, only half the passengers found conveyances, while the other half found themselves ankle-deep in mud and garbage.

And yet, during the time I stayed in a few such towns in my youth, barely making a living by my writing, I formed enduring bonds of friendship. Sometimes I found love. I met men and women of generous spirit, eccentric manner and great fortitude, all of whom have found their way into my stories.

Uninviting and unromantic on first acquaintance, these towns surprised me with small miracles: moonlight on quiet alleys past midnight, for instance. Or the scent of quenched earth and fallen neem leaves after the first rains. Or the happy riot of the weekly bazaar or a mela.

Romance lurks in the most unlikely places.

SHAHJAHANPUR

It is forty-five years since I last saw Shahjahanpur, a sleepy little town halfway between Delhi and Lucknow. I doubt if it has changed much. It wasn't the sort of place...that changes. Even in 1960, when I stopped there for a few hours, it looked as though time had been standing still since the dramatic events of the 1857 uprising, which I described in my novella *A Flight of Pigeons*.

Forty years after those events, in 1896 to be exact, my father had been born in Shahjahanpur's 'military camp', according to Grandfather's army service records. Grandfather's regiment, the Scottish Rifles, must have been quartered there for a few months before moving on to Bareilly, Aligarh, Gorakhpur, Lucknow and other cantonment towns across the hot and dusty Gangetic plains.

This was one reason for me to stop there, but I was also keen to visit the cantonment church, where he had probably been baptized, and where, during the outbreak of 1857, the European residents had been slaughtered. Among the few survivors were

Ruth Labadoor and her mother. Their story came down to me from my father and other sources, and I was keen to follow it up.

The church was still there, of course, but locked up; a memorial to those who had been killed on that fatal day at the end of May stood in the parade ground (I believe it has since been removed); the mango groves and some old bungalows going back to Mutiny days were still evident; and crossing the little Khannant river was the bridge of boats which had played so important a part for those who were escaping from the town—first, the fleeing Europeans; later, the mutineers or their families when the British had retaken the district.

Founded in the seventeenth century, the town had a large Pathan population, and still does. The crowded city area and mohallas are still home to the descendants of Javed Khan, his friends and relatives, and those who had set fire to the cantonment bungalows. In his film of the story, *Junoon*, Shyam Benegal provided a rather opulent-looking Nawabi setting, but in reality Shahjahanpur's streets were occupied by working or lower-middle-class families, and only the Nawab (who lived elsewhere) would have enjoyed much affluence.

The dramatic events of 1857 led to the loss of many innocent lives on both sides of the conflict, Indian and British. In retelling Ruth's story I tried to show how the common humanity of ordinary folk—Hindu, Muslim, or Christian—could sometimes overcome the forces of hate, revenge and retribution.

On a lighter note: The Rose Rum factory stands a little way outside Shahjahanpur. It dates back to pre-Mutiny times. During the uprising it was sacked by rioters. Some quenched their thirst, while others poured barrels of good rum into the Khannant. Grandfather would have been appalled. I don't know if he was much of a drinker, but we did find these verses among his papers. He was, of course, referring to the Solan Brewery near Shimla. Like the Rosa distilleries, it is over 150 years old.

'Where's Solan?' the private was asking;
'Somewhere near Tibet, I should think.'
'There's a brewery there,
And it's brimming with beer,
But we can't get a mouthful to drink!'
So we route-march from Delhi to Solan
In the dust and the maddening sun,
And we're cursing away like Hades
Well knowing there ain't any ladies
To hear every son-of-a-gun!
And when we have climbed up to Solan
Our language continues profane,
For right well we know
We shall soon have to go
Down from Solan to Delhi again!

I'm not sure if Grandfather wrote the poem, but we'll credit it to him anyway—Henry William Bond, with a few profanities edited out by his grandson.

I should add that young Mr Carew, the proprietor of the Rosa distillery, went into hiding and survived the mutiny. If he had not done so, I would not be enjoying Carew's Gin today.

THE BREAK OF MONSOON IN MEERUT

Crossing the Jamuna, still beautiful, before stretches of it came to resemble a huge nullah, the bus took us past a fast-expanding industrial area where a tractor factory was coming up next to a brewery. It was 1962, and I was travelling with my friend Kamal, the two of us having decided to see a bit of Uttar Pradesh. The bus took us across country where General Lake opposed the Maratha forces in 1803 and took Delhi for the British, and over the Hindon river and into UP.

Then north to Meerut, with green fields stretching out on either side: fields of maize, wheat and sugarcane, interspersed with mango orchards and plantations of floating lotus flowers, until we reached the outskirts of the ancient city, got down from the bus, stretched our limbs and climbed onto a cycle rickshaw with our cases and bedding-roll.

The rickshaw boy rode swiftly to the hotel, the only 'English hotel' in Meerut, a building which was probably a barracks at one time, and was owned and managed by a middle-aged

Englishman whom we saw, once, when we blundered into the empty building. Apparently, it wasn't a hotel anymore, but Mr P had never bothered to take the signboard down, and if somebody did turn up, as we had done (this only happened about once a year), then they were welcome to a room and the services of his bearer and of course morning tea and breakfast.

Mr P, who lived alone with his wireless, opened a musty room for us and told us to call for the bearer if we needed anything, or wished to pay our bill. During our two-day stay we never saw him again; he did not emerge from his room, just next to ours; but we heard his radio whenever we cared to listen, mostly relaying BBC cricket commentaries.

Some eighteen miles from Meerut were the remarkable 'Christian' warrior princess Begum Samru's palace and cathedral (she had built both in the very early nineteenth century). We decided to visit them the next day. We took the same rickshaw—the boy attached himself to us for the remainder of our stay—into town on a day so hot and humid that the palace made little impression on me. What does stay in my memory is the restaurant that the rickshaw boy took us to that evening, in the Muslim quarter. It served excellent partridge curry (partridges were plentiful around Meerut) and kebabs. We bought two bottles of beer, which we drank on the verandah back in the hotel, to the crackle and hiss and vaguely military music issuing from Mr P's radio.

Monsoon broke the next day, and my memories of Meerut, ever since, have always been associated with the first rains.

There had been no rain at all for over a month, so the rickshaw boy had told us. Now there were dark clouds overhead, burgeoning with moisture. Thunder blossomed in the air. The dry spell was over. I knew it; the birds knew it; the grass knew it. There was the smell of rain in the air. And the grass, the birds and I responded to this odour with the same sensuous longing. I went out to the balcony, and waited.

A large drop of water hit the railing, darkening the thick dust on the woodwork. A faint breeze had sprung up, and again I felt the moisture, closer and warmer.

Then the rain approached like a dark curtain.

I could see it marching down the street, heavy and remorseless. It drummed on the corrugated tin roof and swept across the road and over the balcony. It swirled with the wind over the trees and roofs of Meerut.

Outside, the street emptied, the crowd dissolved in the rain. Then buses, cars and bullock carts ploughed through the suddenly rushing water. A garland of marigolds, swept off the steps of a temple, came floating down the middle of the road.

The rain stopped as suddenly as it had begun. The day was dying, and the breeze remained cool and moist. In the brief twilight that followed, I was witness to the great yearly flight of insects into the cool brief freedom of the night.

Termites and white ants, which had been sleeping through the hot season, emerged from their lairs. Out of every hole and crack, and from under the roots of trees, huge winged ants emerged, fluttering about heavily on this, the first and last flight of their lives. There was only one direction in which they could fly—towards the light, towards the street lights and the bright neon tubelight above the balcony.

This was the hour of the geckos, the wall lizards. They had their reward for weeks of patient waiting. Plying their sticky tongues, they crammed their stomachs, knowing that such a feast would not come their way again for a long time. Throughout the long hot season the insect world had prepared for this flight out of darkness into light, and the phenomenon would not happen again for another year.

Somewhere, an entire orchestra of frogs began their solemn music. The frogs woke great moths out of a slumber and they flew heavily into the balcony. I went in, shut the windows and got into bed thinking of fireflies flashing messages to each other in the mango groves outside Dehra.

HILL OF THE FAIRIES

Fairy Hill, or Pari Tibba as the paharis call it, is a lonely uninhabited hill, almost a mountain, lying to the east of Mussoorie, at a height of about 6,000 feet. Some nights I have seen a greenish light zigzagging about the hill. Is this 'fairy light' what gives the hill its name? No one has been able to explain it satisfactorily to me; but often from my window I see this strange light.

I have visited Pari Tibba occasionally, scrambling up its rocky slopes where the only paths are the narrow tracks made by goats and the small hill cattle. Rhododendrons and a few stunted oaks are the only trees on the hillsides, but at the summit is a small, grassy plateau ringed by pine trees.

It may have been on this plateau that the early settlers tried building their houses. All their attempts met with failure. The area seemed to attract the worst of any thunderstorm, and several dwellings were struck by lightning and burnt to the ground. People then confined themselves to the adjacent Landour hill, where a flourishing hill station soon grew up.

Why Pari Tibba should be struck so often by lightning has always been something of a mystery to me. Its soil and rock seem no different from the soil or rock of any other mountain in the vicinity. Perhaps a geologist can explain the phenomenon; or perhaps it has something to do with the fairies.

'Why do they call it the Hill of the Fairies?' I asked an old resident, a retired schoolteacher. 'Is the place haunted?'

'So they say,' he said.

'Who say?'

'Oh, people who have heard it's haunted. Some years after the site was abandoned by the settlers, two young runaway lovers took shelter for the night in one of the ruins. There was a bad storm and they were struck by lightning. Their charred bodies were found a few days later. They came from different communities and were buried far from each other, but their spirits hold a tryst every night under the pine trees. You might see them if you're on Pari Tibba after sunset.'

There are no ruins on Pari Tibba, and I can only presume that the building materials were taken away for use elsewhere. And I did not stay on the hill till after sunset. Had I tried climbing downhill in the dark, I would probably have ended up as the third ghost on the mountain. The lovers might have resented my intrusion; or, who knows, they might have welcomed a change. After a hundred years together on a windswept mountain-top, even the most ardent of lovers must tire of each other.

Who could have been seeing ghosts on Pari Tibba after sunset? The nearest resident is a woodcutter who makes charcoal at the bottom of the hill. Terraced fields and a small village straddle the next hill. But the only inhabitants of Pari Tibba are the langurs. They feed on oak leaves and rhododendron buds. The rhododendrons contain intoxicating nectar, and after dining—or wining—to excess, the young monkeys tumble about on the grass in high spirits.

The black bulbuls also feed on the nectar of the rhododendron flower, and perhaps this accounts for the cheekiness of these birds. They are aggressive, disreputable little creatures, who go about in rowdy gangs. The song of most bulbuls consists of several pleasant tinkling notes; but that of the Himalayan black bulbul is as musical as the bray of an ass. Men of science, in their wisdom, have given this bird the sibilant name of *Hypsipetes psaroides*. But the hillmen, in their greater wisdom, call the species the ban bakra, which means the 'jungle goat'.

Perhaps the flowers have something to do with the fairy legend. In April and May, Pari Tibba is covered with the dazzling yellow flowers of St. John's Wort (wort meaning herb). The paharis call the flower a wild rose, and it does resemble one. In Ireland it is called the Rose of Sharon. In Europe this flower is reputed to possess certain magical and curative properties. It is believed to drive away all evil and protect you from witches.

Can St. John's Wort be connected with the fairy legend of Pari Tibba? It is said that most flowers, when they die, become fairies. This might be especially true of St. John's Wort.

There is yet another legend connected with the mountain. A shepherd boy, playing on his flute, discovered a beautiful silver snake basking on a rock. The snake spoke to the boy, saying, 'I was a princess once, but a jealous witch cast a spell over me and turned me into a snake. This spell can only be broken if someone who is pure in heart kisses me thrice. Many years have passed, and I have not been able to find one who is pure in heart.' Then the shepherd boy took the snake in his arms, and he put his lips to its mouth, and at the third kiss he discovered that he was holding a beautiful princess in his arms.

What happened afterwards is anybody's guess.

There are snakes on Pari Tibba, and though they are probably harmless, I have never tried taking one of them in my arms. Once, near a spring, I came upon a checkered water snake. Its body was a series of bulges. I used a stick to exert pressure along the snake's length, and it disgorged five frogs. They came out one after the other, and, to my astonishment, hopped off, little the worse for their harrowing experience. Perhaps they, too, were enchanted. Perhaps shepherd boys, when they kiss the snake-princess, are turned into frogs and remain inside the snake's belly until a writer comes along with a magic stick and releases them from bondage.

Biologists probably have their own explanation for the frogs, but I'm all for perpetuating the fairy legends of Pari Tibba.

THE ROAD TO ANJANI SAIN

Fog, mist, cloud, rain and mildew—these were the things the British must have looked for when selecting suitable sites for the hill stations they set up in the Himalayan foothills 150 years ago: Simla, Mussoorie, Darjeeling, Dalhousie, Nainital, all soggy with monsoon or winter mist and dripping oaks and deodars. The climate must have reminded them of their homes on the English moors or the Scottish highlands.

I have survived all that through the forty or so mountain monsoons that have been thrown at me; and having gone through the annual ritual of wiping the mildew from my books and a certain green fungus from my one and only suit, I decided some years ago to leave cloud country behind for a few days and be the guest of Cyril Raphael, at the Bhuvneshwari Mahila Ashram (a social service organization), at Anjani Sain in Tehri-Garhwal.

Pine country this, dry and bracing, with the scent of pine resin in the air. I have always thought 5,000 to 6,000 feet a healthier altitude to live at, but perhaps I'm prejudiced, having been born in Kasauli, which is pine rather than deodar country. Anjani Sain is about the same height and gets the sun all day. Given adequate food and pure water, it's a healthy place to live. Contrary to what most people think, Garhwal is not a poverty-stricken area. Almost everyone has a bit of land and does at least have the traditional *do-roti* for sustenance, which is more than can be said for the urban unemployed in other parts of northern India. But medical facilities are certainly lacking.

This area has always been known as Khas-patti, probably because it was special in several ways—climate-wise and probably economy-wise too. Down in the flat valley, there are green fields and even mango trees, the descent to lower altitudes being quite sudden in these parts. The small Anjani Sain bazaar, with its single bank, post office, and chemist's shop, shimmers in the noon sun; it looks like a set for a gunfight like in old westerns. But this is, generally, a peaceful area.

At the ashram, I am in time for an early lunch—thick rotis made from *mandwa* (millets)—two of these are more than enough for me! Endless glasses of milky tea will see me through till supper time.

Towering over Anjani Sain, and blessing all those who live or pass beneath, is the Chanderbadni temple, dedicated to one of the incarnations of the goddess Parvati. As this is not one of the main pilgrim routes, the temple does not get as many visitors as some of the other sacred shrines in the hills. Below the Chanderbadni peak is a rest-house, for those who wish to break their journey here.

Anjani Sain lies midway between Tehri and Devprayag—a two-hour bus ride from either place. I came via Tehri, the road climbing steeply above the hot, dusty town that is destined to be submerged by the waters of the Tehri Dam. The dam should have been ready by now, but having been the subject of a great deal of controversy, work on it has progressed in fits and starts.

I am told that this entire region is 'eco-fragile', one of those words bandied around at seminars all, over the world. Well, I am not an expert in these matters, (and who is, I wonder?) but I should think most of our earth is 'eco-fragile', having had to put up with hundreds of thousands of years of human civilization.

Do we stop all development in the name of preserving the environment? Or do we move on regardless? *Proceed with caution* would be the rational person's answer. But are human beings really rational?

Old Tehri was no beauty spot, and New Tehri (growing rapidly above it), is even uglier; from a distance it looks like a giant cemetery.

When the architecture of suburban Delhi is brought to the hills, what is there to say? You just look the other way.

Fortunately the defaced mountain is soon left behind, and as it slips out of sight and we ascend into the pine regions, the eye is soothed by the pretty, slate-covered houses of the villages and their little gardens ablaze with marigolds and yellow and bronze chrysanthemums.

Chrysanthemums love this climate. Down in the fields there are patches of crimson *cholai* (amaranth) interspersed with the fresh green of young wheat.

And here be leopards! My companion tells me of one that strolls down the motor road every evening, forcing the local bus to go around him. His presence also accounts for the absence of stray dogs. '

Suddenly in the distance I see what at first glance appears to be a cloud or a large white sailing ship. On approaching, it turns out to be the freshly white-washed buildings of the Bhuvneshwari Mahila Ashram, clinging to the steep slopes of the mountain.

Here, for two or three days, I find rest and sustenance. The manifold activities of the ashram, (directed mainly towards the welfare of widows and small children) are there for all to see, and I recall the relief work undertaken by its young field workers after the Uttarkashi earthquake last year—they had rushed to the area before the government agencies could swing into action.

However, as a social worker I am somewhat inept. I am just a frazzled old writer who now seeks a refuge from the all-pervasive clutter of tourism that makes ordinary life almost impossible in our hill stations.

I hope the land-grabbers and the real estate 'developers' never get this far. They are welcome to their malls and artificial lakes and concrete parks. Just so long as I am free to escape from it all, to sit here at Anjani Sain contemplating a large white rose in Cyril's garden, while the rest of the world watches video.

THE MAGIC OF TUNGNATH

The mountains and valleys of Garhwal never fail to spring surprises on the traveller in search of the picturesque. It is impossible to know every corner of the Himalayas, which means that there are always new corners to discover; forest or meadow, mountain stream or wayside shrine.

The temple of Tungnath, at a little over 12,000 ft, is the highest shrine on the inner Himalayan range. It lies just below the Chandrashila peak. Some way off the main pilgrim routes, it is less frequented than Kedarnath or Badrinath, although it forms a part of the Kedar temple establishment. The priest here is a local man, a Brahmin from the village of Maku; the other Kedar temples have South Indian priests, a tradition begun by Sankaracharya, the eighth-century Hindu reformer and revivalist.

Tungnath's lonely eminence gives it a magic of its own. To get there (or beyond it), one passes through some of the most delightful temperate forests in the Garhwal Himalayas. Pilgrim or trekker or just plain rambler, such as myself, one comes away a better man, forest-refreshed and more aware of what the earth was really like before mankind began to strip it bare.

Duiri Tal, a small lake, lies cradled on the hill above Ukhimath at a height of 8,000 ft. It was the favourite spot of one of Garhwal's earliest British Commissioners, J.H. Batten, whose administration continued for twenty years (1836–56). He wrote:

> The day I reached there it was snowing and young trees were laid prostrate under the weight of snow, the lake was frozen over to a depth of about two inches. There was no human habitation, and the place looked a veritable wilderness. The next morning when the sun appeared, the Chaukhamba and many other peaks extending as far as Kedarnath seemed covered with a new quilt of snow as if close at hand. The whole scene was so exquisite that one could not tire of gazing at it for hours. I think a person who has a subdued settled despair in his mind would all of a sudden feel a kind of bounding and exalting cheerfulness which will be imparted to his frame by the atmosphere of Duiri Tal.

This feeling of uplift can be experienced almost anywhere along the Tungnath range. Duiri Tal is still some way way off the beaten track, and anyone wishing to spend the night there should carry a tent; but further along this range, the road ascends to Dugalbeta (at about 9,000 ft) where a PWD rest house, gaily painted, has come up like some exotic orchid in the midst of a lush meadow topped by excelsia pines and pencil cedars. Many an official who has stayed here has rhapsodized on the charms of Dugalbeta; and if you are unofficial (and therefore not entitled to stay in the bungalow), you can move on to Chopta, lusher still, where there is accommodation of a sort for pilgrims and other hardy souls. Two or three little tea-shops provide mattresses and quilts. The Garhwal Mandal Vikas Nigam has put up a rest house. These tourist rest houses, scattered over the length and breadth of Garhwal, are a great boon to travellers; but during the pilgrims season (May/June), they are filled to overflowing, and if you turn up unexpectedly, you might have to take your pick of tea-shop or 'dharamsala', something of a lucky dip, since they vary a good deal in comfort and cleanliness.

The trek from Chopta to Tungnath is only three and a half miles, but in that distance one ascends about 3,000 ft and the pilgrim may be forgiven for feeling that at places he is on a perpendicular path. Like a ladder to heaven, I couldn't help thinking.

In spite of its steepness, my companion, the redoubtable climber Ganesh Saili, insisted that we take a short cut. After clawing our way up tufts of alpine grass, which formed the rungs of our ladder, we were stuck and had to inch our way down again, so that the ascent of Tungnath began to resemble a game of Snakes and Ladders.

A tiny guardian-temple dedicated to Lord Ganesh surprised on top. Nor was I really fatigued; for the cold fresher air and the verdant greenery surrounding us was like an intoxicant. Myriads of wild flowers grew on the open slopes—buttercups, anemones, wild strawberries, forget-me-nots, rock-cross, enough to rival Bhyunders' Valley of Flowers at this time of the year.

But before reaching these alpine meadows, we climb through a rhododendron forest, and here one finds at least three species of this flower: the red-flowering tree rhododendron (found throughout the Himalayas between 6,000 ft and 10,000 ft); a second variety, the Almatta, with flowers that are light red or rosy in colour; and the third, Chimul or white variety, found at heights ranging between 10,000 ft and 13,000 ft. The Chimul is a brushwood, seldom more than twelve feet high and growing slantingly due to the heavy burden of snow it has to carry for almost six months in a year.

The brushwood rhododendrons are the last trees on our ascent, for as we approach Tungnath, the treeline ends and there is nothing between the earth and the sky except grass and rock and tiny flowers. Above us, a couple of crows dive-bomb a hawk, who does his best to escape their attentions. Crows are the world's great survivors. They are capable of living at any height and in any climate; as much at home in the back streets of Delhi as on the heights of Tungnath.

Another surviver, up here at any rate, is the Pika, a sort of mouse-hare, who looks neither like a mouse nor a hare but rather like a tiny guinea-pig; small ears, no tail, grey-brown fur and chubby feet. They emerge from their holes under the rock to forage for grasses on which to feed. Their simple diet and thick fur enable them to live in extreme cold, and they have been found at 16,000 ft, which is higher than where any mammal lives. The Garhwalis call this little creature the Runda—at any rate, that's what the temple priest called it, adding that it was not averse to entering houses and helping itself to grain and other delicacies. So perhaps there's more in it of mouse than of hare.

These little Rundas were with us all the way from Chopta to Tungnath, peering out from their rocks or scampering about on the hillside, seemingly unconcerned by our presence. At Tungnath they live beneath the temple flagstones. The priest's grandchildren were having a game discovering their burrows;

the Rundas would go in at one hole and pop at another; they must have had a system of underground passages.

When we arrived, clouds had gathered over Tungnath, as they do almost every afternoon. The temple looked austere in the gathering gloom.

To some, the name 'tung' indicates 'lofty', from the position of the temple on the highest peak outside the main chain of the Himalayas; others derive it from the word 'tangna'—'to be suspended'—in allusion to the form under which the deity is worshipped here. The form is the Swayambhu Ling; and on Shivratri or the night of Shiva, the true believer may, 'with the eye of faith', see the lingam increase in size; but 'to the evil-minded no such favour is granted'.

The temple, though not very large, is certainly impressive, mainly because of its setting and the solid slabs of grey granite from which it is built. The whole place somehow reminds me of Emily Bronte's *Wuthering Heights*—bleak, wind-swept, open to the skies. And as you look down from the temple at the little half-deserted hamlet that serves it in summer, the eye is met by grey slate roofs and piles of stones, with just a few hardy souls in residence, for the majority of pilgrims now prefer to spend the night down at Chopta.

Even the temple priest, attended by his son and grandsons, complains bitterly of cold. To spend every day barefoot on those cold flagstones must indeed be a hardship. I wince after five minutes of it, made worse by stepping into a puddle of icy water. I shall never make a good pilgrim; no reward for me in this world or the next. But the pandit's feet are literally thick-skinned, and the children seem oblivious to the cold. Still, in October they must be happy to descend to Maku, their home village on the slopes below Dugalbeta.

It begins to rain as we leave the temple. We pass herds of sheep huddled in the ruined dharamsala. The crows are still rushing about the grey weeping skies, although the hawk has very sensibly gone away. A Runda sticks his nose out from his hole, probably to take a look at the weather. There is a clap of thunder and he disappears, like the white rabbit in *Alice in Wonderland*. We are halfway down the Tungnath 'ladder' when it begins to rain quite heavily. And now we pass our first genuine pilgrims, a group of intrepid Bengalis who are heading straight into the storm. They are without umbrellas or raincoats, but they are not to be deterred.

Oaks and rhododendrons flash past as we dash down the steep, winding path. Another short cut, and rock-climber Ganesh Saili takes a tumble, but is cushioned by moss and buttercups. My wristwatch strikes a rock and the glass is shattered. No matter. Time here is of little or no significance. Away with time! Is this, I wonder, the 'bounding and exciting cheerfulness' experienced by Batten and now manifesting itself in me?

The tea-shop beckons. How would one manage in the hills without these wayside tea-shops? Miniature inns, they provide food, shelter and even lodging to dozens at a time.

We sit on a bench between a Gujar herdsman and a pilgrim who is too feverish to make the climb to the temple. He accepts my offer of an aspirin to go with his tea. We tackle some buns—rock-hard, to match our environment—and wash the pellets down with hot sweet tea.

There is a small shrine here, too, right in front of the tea-shop. It is a slab or rock roughly shaped like a lingam, and it is daubed with vermilion and strewn with offerings of wild flowers. The mica in the rock gives it a beautiful sheen.

I suppose Hinduism comes closest to being a nature religion.

Rivers, rocks, trees, plants, animals and birds, all play their part, both in mythology and in everyday worship. This harmony is most evident in these remote places, where god and mountains coexist. Tungnath, as yet unspoilt by a materialistic society, exerts its magic on all who come here with open mind and heart.

SOME HILL STATION GHOSTS

Shimla has its phantom-rickshaw and Lansdowne its headless horseman. Mussoorie has its woman in white. Late at night, she can be seen sitting on the parapet wall on the winding road up to the hill station. Don't stop to offer her a lift. She will fix you with her evil eye and ruin your holiday.

The Mussoorie taxi drivers and other locals call her Bhoot Aunty. Everyone has seen her at some time or the other. To give her a lift is to court disaster. Many accidents have been attributed to her baleful presence. And when people pick themselves up from the road (or are picked up by concerned citizens), Bhoot Aunty is nowhere to be seen, although survivors swear that she was in the car with them.

Ganesh Saili, Abha and I were coming back from Dehradun late one night when we saw this woman in white sitting on the parapet by the side of the road. As our headlights fell on her, she turned her face away, Ganesh, being a thorough gentleman, slowed down and offered her a lift. She turned towards us then, and smiled a wicked smile. She seemed quite attractive except that her canines protruded slightly in vampire fashion.

'Don't stop!' screamed Abha. 'Don't even look at her! It's Aunty!'

Ganesh pressed down on the accelerator and sped past her. Next day we heard that a tourist's car had gone off the road and the occupants had been severely injured. The accident took place shortly after they had stopped to pick up a woman in white who had wanted a lift. But she was not among the injured.

◆

Miss Ripley-Bean, an old English lady who was my neighbour when I lived near Wynberg-Allen school, told me that her family was haunted by a malignant phantom head that always appeared before the death of one of her relatives.

She said her brother saw this apparition the night before her mother died, and both she and her sister saw it before the death of their father. The sister slept in the same room. They were both awakened one night by a curious noise in the cupboard facing their beds. One of them began getting out of bed to see if their cat was in the room, when the cupboard door suddenly opened and a luminous head appeared. It was covered with matted hair and appeared to be in an advanced stage of decomposition. Its fleshless mouth grinned at the terrified sisters. And then as they crossed themselves, it vanished. The next day they learned that their father, who was in Lucknow, had died suddenly, at about the time that they had seen the death's head.

◆

Everyone likes to hear stories about haunted houses; even sceptics will listen to a ghost story, while casting doubts on its veracity.

Rudyard Kipling wrote a number of memorable ghost stories set in India—*Imray's Return, The Phantom Rickshaw, The Mark of the Beast, The End of the Passage*—his favourite milieu being the haunted dak bungalow. But it was only after his return to England that he found himself actually having to live in a haunted house. He writes about it in his autobiography, *Something of Myself.*

> The spring of '96 saw us in Torquay, where we found a house for our heads that seemed almost too good to be true. It was large and bright, with big rooms each and all open to the sun, the ground embellished with great trees and the warm land dipping southerly to the clean sea under the Mary Church cliffs. It had been inhabited for thirty years by three old maids.
>
> The revelation came in the shape of a growing depression which enveloped us both—a gathering blackness of mind and sorrow of the heart, that each put down to the new, soft climate and, without telling the other, fought against for long weeks. It was the Feng-shui—the Spirit of the house itself—that darkened the sunshine and fell upon us every time we entered, checking the very words on our lips... We paid forfeit and fled. More than thirty years later we returned down the steep little road to that house, and found, quite unchanged, the same brooding spirit of deep despondency within the rooms.

Again, thirty years later, he returned to this house in his short story, 'The House Surgeon', in which two sisters cannot come to terms with the suicide of a third sister, and brood upon the tragedy day and night until their thoughts saturate every room of the house.

Many years ago, I had a similar experience in a house in

Dehradun, in which an elderly English couple had died from neglect and starvation. In 1947, when many European residents were leaving the town and emigrating to the UK, this poverty-stricken old couple, sick and friendless, had been forgotten. Too ill to go out for food or medicine, they had died in their beds, where they were discovered several days later by the landlord's munshi.

The house stood empty for several years. No one wanted to live in it. As a young man, I would sometimes roam about the neglected grounds or explore the cold, bare rooms, now stripped of furniture, doorless and windowless, and I would be assailed by a feeling of deep gloom and depression. Of course I knew what had happened there, and that may have contributed to the effect the place had on me. But when I took a friend, Jai Shankar, through the house, he told me he felt quite sick with apprehension and fear. 'Ruskin, why have you brought me to this awful house?' he said. 'I'm sure it's haunted.' And only then did I tell him about the tragedy that had taken place within its walls.

Today, the house is used as a government office. No one lives in it at night except for a Gurkha chowkidar, a man of strong nerves who sleeps in the back verandah. The atmosphere of the place doesn't bother him, but he does hear strange sounds in the night. 'Like someone crawling about on the floor above,' he tells me. 'And someone groaning. These old houses are noisy places...'

◆

A morgue is not a noisy place, as a rule. And for a morgue attendant, corpses are silent companions.

Old Mr Jacob, who lives just behind the cottage, was once

a morgue attendant for the local mission hospital. In those days it was situated at Sunny Bank, about a hundred metres up the hill from here. One of the outhouses served as the morgue: Mr Jacob begs me not to identify it.

He tells me of a terrifying experience he went through when he was doing night duty at the morgue.

'The body of a young man was found floating in the Aglar River, behind Landour, and was brought to the morgue while I was on night duty. It was placed on the table and covered with a sheet.

'I was quite accustomed to seeing corpses of various kinds and did not mind sharing the same room with them, even after dark. On this occasion a friend had promised to join me, and to pass the time I strolled around the room, whistling a popular tune. I think it was "Danny Boy", if I remember right. My friend was a long time coming, and I soon got tired of whistling and sat down on the bench beside the table. The night was very still, and I began to feel uneasy. My thoughts went to the boy who had drowned and I wondered what he had been like when he was alive. Dead bodies are so impersonal...

The morgue had no electricity, just a kerosene lamp, and after some time I noticed that the flame was very low. As I was about to turn it up, it suddenly went out. I lit the lamp again, after extending the wick. I returned to the bench, but I had not been sitting there for long when the lamp again went out, and something moved very softly and quietly past me.

I felt quite sick and faint, and could hear my heart pounding away. The strength had gone out of my legs, otherwise I would have fled from the room. I felt quite weak and helpless, unable even to call out.

Presently the footsteps came nearer and nearer. Something

cold and icy touched one of my hands and felt its way up towards my neck and throat. It was behind me, then it was before me. Then it was *over* me. I was in the arms of the corpse!

I must have fainted, because when I woke up I was on the floor, and my friend was trying to revive me. The corpse was back on the table.'

'It may have been a nightmare,' I suggested. 'Or you allowed your imagination to run riot.'

'No,' said Mr Jacobs. 'There were wet, slimy marks on my clothes. And the feet of the corpse matched the wet footprints on the floor.'

After this experience, Mr Jacobs refused to do any more night duty at the morgue.

◆

From Herbertpur near Paonta you can go up to Kalsi, and then up the hill road to Chakrata.

Chakrata is in a security zone, most of it off limits to tourists, which is one reason why it has remained unchanged in 150 years of its existence. This small town's population of 1,500 is the same today as it was in 1947—probably the only town in India that hasn't shown a population increase.

Courtesy a government official, I was fortunate enough to be able to stay in the forest rest house on the outskirts of the town. This is a new building, the old rest house—a little way downhill—having fallen into disuse. The chowkidar told me the old rest house was haunted, and that this was the real reason for its having been abandoned. I was a bit sceptical about this, and asked him what kind of haunting took place in it. He told me that he had himself gone through a frightening experience in the old house, when he had gone there to light a fire for some forest officers who were expected that night. After lighting the fire, he looked round and saw a large black animal, like a wild cat, sitting on the wooden floor and gazing into the fire. 'I called out to it, thinking it was someone's pet. The creature turned, and looked full at me with eyes that were human, and a face which was the face of an ugly woman. The creature snarled at me, and the snarl became an angry howl. Then it vanished!'

'And what did you do?' I asked.

'I vanished too,' said the chowkidar. I haven't been down to that house again.'

I did not volunteer to sleep in the old house but made myself comfortable in the new one, where I hoped I would not be troubled by any phantom. However, a large rat kept me company, gnawing away at the woodwork of a chest of drawers. Whenever I switched on the light it would be silent, but as soon as the light was off, it would start gnawing away again.

This reminded me of a story old Miss Kellner (of my Dehra childhood) told me, of a young man who was desperately in love with a girl who did not care for him. One day, when he was following her in the street, she turned on him and, pointing to a rat which some boys had just killed, said, 'I'd as soon marry that rat as marry you.' He took her cruel words so much to heart that he pined away and died. After his death the girl was haunted at night by a rat and occasionally she would be bitten. When the family decided to emigrate, they travelled down to Bombay in order to embark on a ship sailing for London. The ship had just left the quay, when shouts and screams were heard from the pier. The crowd scattered, and a huge rat with fiery eyes ran down to the end of the quay. It sat there, screaming with rage, then jumped into the water and disappeared. After that (according to Miss Kellner), the girl was not haunted again.

Old dak bungalows and forest rest houses have a reputation for being haunted. And most hill stations have their resident ghosts—and ghost writers! But I will not extend this catalogue of ghostly hauntings and visitations, as I do not want to discourage tourists from visiting Landour and Mussoorie. In some countries, ghosts are an added attraction for tourists. Britain boasts of hundreds of haunted castles and stately homes, and visitors to Romania seek out Transylvania and Dracula's castle. So do we promote Bhoot Aunty as a tourist attraction? Only if she reforms and stops sending vehicles off those hairpin bends that lead to Mussoorie.

AWAY FROM HOME

Wears and upheavals destroy lives, but it is always worth remembering that life and humanity are bigger than them. We hear of heroic stands and superhuman perseverance, but fortitude and resilience are usually found in mundane things and are easily missed.

It was in Jersey, in UK's Channel Islands, that I first realized this. I was there for a year in the early 1950s. It was a quiet and very law-abiding island. Even through the German occupation during World War II, the islanders had gone about their business—mostly fishing and growing tomatoes—without paying much heed to the occupying power. And when the war ended in Europe, the Germans simply melted away and the islanders carried on growing their tomatoes. It was as though nothing had happened.

◆

There are memories that we fear and run away from all our lives. But we also find solace in memory, often in unexpected ways, as unbidden images return from our past.

When I was living in London as a young man in the 1950s, I was homesick and miserable, separated by a thousand miles of ocean, plain and desert from my beloved Himalayas. And then one morning the depressing London fog became a mountain mist, and the sound of traffic became the *hoo-hoo-hoo* of the wind in the branches of tall deodar trees.

I remembered a little mountain path from my boyhood which led my restless feet into a cool forest of oak and rhododendron, and then on to the windswept crest of a naked hilltop. The hill was called Cloud's End. It commanded a view of the plains on one side, and of the snow peaks on the other. Little silver rivers twisted across the valley below, where the rice fields formed a patchwork of emerald green.

During the rains, clouds enveloped the valley but left the hill alone, an island in the sky. Wild sorrel grew among the rocks, and there were many flowers—convolvulus, clover, wild begonia, dandelion—sprinkling the hillside. On the spur of the hill stood the ruins of an old brewery. The roof had long since disappeared and the rain had beaten the stone floors smooth and yellow. Some enterprising Englishman had spent a lifetime here making beer for his thirsty compatriots down in the plains. Now, moss and ferns grew from the walls. In a hollow beneath a flight of worn steps, a wildcat had made its home. It was a beautiful grey creature, black-striped, with pale green eyes. Sometimes it watched me from the steps or the wall, but it never came near.

No one lived on the hill, except occasionally a coal burner in a temporary grass-thatched hut. But villagers used the path, grazing their sheep and cattle on the grassy slopes. Each cow or sheep had a bell suspended from its neck, to let the shepherd boy know of its whereabouts. The boy could then lie in the sun and eat wild strawberries without fear of losing his animals.

I remembered some of the shepherd boys and girls.

There was a boy who played a flute. Its rough, sweet, straightforward notes travelled clearly across the mountain air. He would greet me with a nod of his head, without taking the flute from his lips. There was a girl who was nearly always cutting grass for fodder. She wore heavy bangles on her feet, and long silver earrings. She did not speak much either, but she always had a wide grin on her face when she met me on the path. She used to sing to herself, or to the sheep, or to the grass, or to the sickle in her hand.

•

It was March 1955 and I was returning to India, to everything I had missed keenly during my three years in the UK. Although I was twenty-one, and had been earning my own living for over three years, in many ways I was still a boy, with a boy's thoughts and dreams—dreams of romance and high adventure and good companionship. And I was still a lonely boy, alone on that big ship—passengers and crew all strangers to me—still sailing to an uncertain future.

I had two books with me—Thoreau's *Walden* and Richard Jefferies's *The Story of My Heart*—both reflecting my burgeoning interest in the natural world—but during the day the cabin was hot and stuffy, and the decks too crowded, so I postponed most of my reading until the journey was over. But at night, when it was cool on deck, and most of the passengers were down below, watching a film or drinking Polish vodka (it was a Polish ship), I would sit out under the stars while the ship ploughed on through the Red Sea. There was no sound but the dull thunder of the ship's screws and the faint tinkle of music from an open porthole.

And as I sat there, pondering on my future, a line from Thoreau kept running through my head. 'Why should I feel lonely? Is not our planet in the Milky Way?'

Wherever I went, the stars were there to keep me company. And I knew that as long as I responded, in both a physical and mystical way, to the natural world—sea, sun, earth, moon and stars—I would never feel lonely upon this planet.

SOUNDS OF THE SEA

For years I had this large sea-shell, and by putting it to my ear I could hear the distant sob and hiss of the sea—or so I fancied, until this romantic notion was dispelled by twelve-year-old Mukesh, who told me that the same effect could be obtained by holding an empty cup to my ear. He was right, of course. In fact, the cup sounds better than the shell! And for years I'd gone on imagining that the sound of the sea was somehow trapped in my shell.... But I still cling to it, for it takes me back to Jamnagar, on the west coast of India, and memories of sea and sand, small steamers and large Arab dhows plying across the Gulf of Kutch.

My small hand in my father's, I explored with him the little port's harbour and beach, bringing home shells of considerable variety, and even, on one occasion, a small crab, which lived in a spare bathtub for several days and was forgotten—until a visiting aunt, deciding on a tub-bath after a long train journey, found it keeping her company among the soap-suds. Amidst much clamour and consternation, it was evicted from the house and dropped into a nearby well. But my aunt was convinced that I had deliberately placed it in the tub, and refused to speak to me for the rest of her stay.

A small British steamer was often in port, and my father and I would visit the captain, a good-natured Welshman who gave me chocolates, a great treat in those days, for Jamnagar was too small a place for a Western confectionery shop. I was ready to go to sea with Captain Jenkins, convinced that chocolates were only to be found on tramp steamers.

We left Jamnagar when the Second World War broke out and my father joined the RAF. It was to be some ten years before I saw the sea again, for I went to boarding school in the hills. I was still in my teens, but now bereft of my father, when I set sail from Bombay in the *S. S. Strathnaver*, a beautiful P&O liner, one of a fleet, its sister ships being the *Strathaird* and *Stratheden*. Those were the days of the big passenger liners, before fast air travel put an end to leisurely ocean voyages. It took just over a fortnight to reach Southampton or London, but there was never a dull moment on the voyage. Apart from interesting shipboard acquaintances—the sort of mixed company that gave Somerset Maugham material for his stories—there were also colourful ports of call: Aden, Port Said, Marseilles, Gibraltar. At Marseilles, I decided to miss the coach-tour and instead walk into the town. After three hours of walking along miles and miles of dockland, I finally reached the outskirts of the city—just in time to catch the coach back to the ship!

But later, living in London, I never tired of walking among the docks and wharfs along the Thames, for many of those places were associated with the novels of Dickens, which had inspired me to become a writer. Limehouse, Wapping, Shadwell

Stairs, the Mile End Road, the East India Docks, these were all places I knew from *Bleak House, Dombey and Son*, and *Our Mutual Friend*. And there was the fog, a thick peasouper, that seemed to have lingered on from the fog that had enveloped the characters and the action in *Bleak House*, setting the tone for that masterpiece. London, I am told, no longer has fogs—they are dispersed by modern and scientific means—and although the air no doubt is cleaner and healthier now, I feel sure some of the magic has gone—along with the East End of old.

From London's dockland to the Channel Islands was a short trip but a considerable change. I lived on the island of Jersey for two years. It had a number of bays and inlets of great charm and beauty, and it was here that I learnt to watch the tides advancing and retreating, and discovered that the tides make different sounds in different places.

Every tide has its own music, and those who live near lonely shores soon learn to recognize the familiar ripple, throb, sob or sigh. And sometimes the tide comes up from the deep against four steep sand-bank and roars defiance.

The tide-rip which pushes through the Channel Islands off the Norman coast has a smoother thud than most, though it comes from the same Atlantic as the harsher-sounding waters among the Orkneys. The difference may be that the channel tides move through purple waters which have drifted up from sunny Portugal, while the other has a shiver from the coast of Greenland.

The music of sea waters is wonderfully varied. Every bay and headland and strait has its note which the local fisherfolk recognize even in time of dense fog; a note which guides them home or which helps them locate the place for their fishing.

For many years I have been living far from the sea. Sometimes

I feel the urge to go down to the sea again, all the way from the Himalayas to Cape Comorin. And maybe I will one day.

Meanwhile, if I wish to listen to the sound of the sea, there's always my sea-shell—or Mukesh's tea-cup.

MY TWO YEARS IN LONDON

I was lonely in London.

Living alone in a big city, working in an office from nine to five, and coming back to a gas-fire in an empty bed-sitting room, was not what I wanted out of life. I'd go out to eat in a small café, then return to my room, put a sheet of paper into my small portable typewriter, and type out a page or two of my novel. It was into its second draft. And there would be a third before it finally found favour with its eventual publisher.

Diana Athill, my publisher's editor, was kind and helpful. The people in the Photax Office, where I worked, were kind and friendly. My landlady was kind and solicitous. Or I should say landladies, because I had at least three of them, one after another—Belsize Park, Haverstock Hill, Swiss Cottage—all Jewish landladies, widows I think, who never troubled or scolded me if I came in late or played my radio too loudly. One of them gave me breakfast in my room. Scrambled eggs, occasionally with peppers. This helped sustain me, because for lunch—at a snackbar near the office—it was almost always baked beans on toast, the cheapest item on their menu.

People were kind,
But I was lonely,
I had no companions of my own age.

So I went to the pictures. And once a month to the theatre. And I dropped at Foyles and bought old books. And I came home to my empty room, lit the gas-fire and worked on my book.

After about six months on my own, I found I was losing vision in my right eye. It was as though I was looking at the world through a shifting cloud. I took vitamins, they had been 'discovered' only recently—and experimented with various eye-drops—but the cloud only got darker and denser. So I went to a doctor, who said it needed further investigation and got me admitted to the Hampstead General Hospital. There, various specialists came to see me. One said I was suffering from malnutrition; true enough. Another said I had Eales' disease, a rare condition of the retina. A third felt it had something to do with a sluggish liver. (I'd suffered from jaundice in the past.) Tests showed that my intestines were full of amoebiasis, no doubt brought with me from India, and I was put on a course of emetine injections, which made me feel awful. Then my eye, or rather retina, was photographed by a high intensity camera, and the resultant picture appeared in a medical journal. (Not my picture, only the eye's; I had to wait a few years before my own mugshot appeared in a newspaper.)

Once the amoeba had been vanquished, I (or rather my sick eye), was given cortisone injections, cortisone then being the wonder drug that was supposed to clear up all sorts of intractable conditions. This left my poor eye looking rather bloody and fierce, prompting one fellow patient to remark that I could have passed for *The Phantom of the Opera*.

Weakened by the emitine and various laxatives, I found myself too weak to even get up in order to visit the loo, so I was given the privilege of having a bed-pan. This occasioned some raillery from the others in the ward (it was a general ward with about twenty beds), who labelled me the B-P Superman—the Bed-pan Superman, after the British Petroleum Superman who was on all the hoardings.

I did improve rapidly, and was soon making the rounds of the ward, interviewing the other patients like a doctor on the rounds, quizzing them on their ailments and recommending purgatives and the bed-pan.

The book trolley came the rounds every day, and I read a book a day, discovering the stories of William Saroyan (*My Name is Aram* and *The Humans Comedy*), Denton Welch (*A Voice Through a Cloud*) and Josephine Tey (*The Daughter of Time*).

Saroyan had grown up in an Armenian immigrant community in California, and in his stories he captured the essence of small-town life in his part of the world. He won the Pulitzer Prize for his play, *The Time of Your Life*, and was very popular in the 1940s and '50s, but most of his work is now out of print.

Denton Welch was a promising young English writer who had a tragic accident while riding his bicycle on a country road. He was knocked down and run over by a lorry. For over a year, he lingered between life and death, and during this period he managed to write his very moving account of his struggle to recover. He succumbed to his many injuries. I hope *A Voice Through a Cloud* is reprinted some day. His earlier travel book, *Maiden Voyage*, should also be revisted.

Josephine Tey wrote several detective novels during her short life. In *The Daughter of Time,* the novel I read in my hospital bed, her detective, Inspector Grant, finds himself in a hospital bed and passes the time by trying to reconstruct the murder of the princes in the tower, and with the help of his research assistant proves that it was King Henry VII and not King Richard III who was responsible for their deaths. A historical who-done-it, resolved without moving from the hospital bed. No fast-paced action, but suspenseful all the same.

How sad it is that such fine writers have been neglected or forgotten. Time and changing fashions take their toll on the best talents. Only a handful survive.

Sometimes short stories have a better chance of survival, because the good ones get picked-up for inclusions in anthologies, and then get selected again and again. One of my earliest short stories, 'The Eyes Have It', is still turning up in anthologies and school readers, fifty years after it was first written. But once a novel goes out of print, it is hard to revive it. And novels date very quickly. Sometimes too much extraneous matter goes into them, whereas the best short stories stick to the essentials.

When I wrote *The Room on the Roof* I had published only two or three short stories, so what was I, still a pimply and skinny youth, doing, trying to write a novel?

In a way it was a mistake, because in writing it I used up all the experience I had of life and was left with nothing for a second novel!

But it had to be written.

That last year in Dehra, before I left for England, was now so ingrained in me, so much a part of my emotional make-up, that it had to be expressed in the way I knew best—the written word. The journal had become a novel, and some, Krishan,

Meena and the rest stayed alive for me on the printed page. Though it might never have been published and I couldn't be sure of this during the four years that various drafts shuttled between me and Andre Deutsch's editor, Diana Athill, the thing had been done, the catharsis had completed, and I could think of other people, other loves, and try something different.

My editor, Diana Athill, was then a young woman in her thirties. Many years later she was to become quite a celebrity, the author of several successful autobiographies, which were frank, revealing and beautifully written. But when I knew her she hadn't done any writing (or none that I know of), although she was very busy assessing and introducing the work of many promising young writers, novelists such as Jack Kerouac and V.S. Naipaul. Although she did not (could not) teach me how to write (I stubbornly refused to temper my addiction to semi-commas and certain Indianisms), she made me feel that I was part of her literary world, giving me gossip about others writers and telling me about the books they were publishing. I visited her at her flat in Regent's Park quite often, and even took her to see an Indian picture, *Aan* (the first to get a commercial release in London) but it was a terrible let-down, a very silly film, the sort of Bombay extravaganza that gave a completely misleading and over-romanticized conception of Indians. I felt more at ease introducing her to paan at a little Indian restaurant near Fitzroy Square, but I'm afraid she didn't care much for paan either. My efforts to make Diana an Indophile were not very successful. But she liked my book. 'I can see why you love India,' she said, 'It's so easy to make friends.'

But my first appearance in print (in London, that is) really came about as a result of my lengthy stay in the Hampstead General Hospital. A fellow patient, an English boy of about my age (perhaps a little younger) turned out to be a good reader, and when he was discharged he gave me a copy of a magazine for teenagers called *Young Elizabethan*. A couple of months later, when I was back at my typewriter, I sent them one of my short stories. It was published, and paid for. And even after I had returned to India I continued to write for the *Elizabethan*, and several of my early stories appeared in it—'The Thief,' 'The Long Day', 'The Big Race,' 'The Stolen Daffodils,' among others—until it closed down around 1959.

And while still in that hospital bed, I had written a piece called 'My Two Homes'—about an English boy growing up in an Indian home—and this became a talk that I gave on BBC Radio. The BBC's Home Service also ran a weekly short story programme, and when I returned to India and started freelancing, many of my early stories found a home with them. 'The Night Train at Deoli', 'The Woman on Platform 8' and many others were read by Robert Rietti, a fine actor in radio plays. Back in Dehra, I would drop in on a friend who had a short-wave radio, and listened spellbound to my stories being beamed to me from distant London.

So my two years in London were a good preparation for the years of struggle that lay ahead, when I returned to India. Although my job was a dull one, I did find time to write, to read, to visit the theatre, to wander about the streets of London (getting to know that city fairly well), and so banishing the loneliness that awaited me whenever I returned to cold bed-sitting room.

And there were friends too. Students, mostly, who came in and out of my life at random.

Praven, a Gujarati boy who was a little younger than me; he liked visiting pubs and night clubs! I had no idea what he was studying—I never saw him with a book—but he was the recipient of regular remittances from his father in Bombay.

Thanh, a Vietnamese, who cultivated me because he wanted to 'improve his English', he dropped me when he discovered I spoke English with an Indian accent.

Vu-phuong, also Vietnamese, who used to tell me my fortune with tea-leaves. When you finish drinking your tea, you let the tea-leaves settle naturally, and the pattern they form gives you an indication of what to expect in the future. This was great fun, because it meant sharing innumerable cups of tea with Vu, with whom I fell in love. But when I asked her to marry me, she said it was not in the tea-leaves.

Just as well, perhaps. If I'd been married in England (or Vietnam), I might never have returned to India.

And returning to India was still very much my first priority.

But first I had to save a little money, publish my novel, and try to see a little better with my right eye.

The best way to get to know a city is to walk all over the place. So I walked all over Soho and the West End; I walked from Primrose Hill down to Baker Street, looking for Sherlock Holmes, but couldn't find him; I walked all over the East End, looking for places described by Dickens in *Oliver Twist* and *Our Mutual Friend*, but they looked very different from what I'd imagined; I walked around Kensington Gardens, looking for Peter Pan, but he must have been away in Neverland. So I went to Kew Gardens, and felt quite at home in a big glass hothouse, surrounded by tropical plants of every description, after that, whenever I felt homesick, I went down to Kew—not just in lilac time, but any time…

Andre Deutsch finally gave me a £50 advance for *The Room on the Roof*. I did not wait for it to be published, but bought a ticket to Bombay for £40; gave a week's notice to my kind employers, who presented me with a travel bag; and boarded the *M.S. Batory* at Southampton, accompanied by said travel bag and an old suitcase bulging with books and a few clothes. It was March, 1955, and I was twenty-one years old. I had left India to seek my fortune in the West; and now I was returning to the East to find, if not fortune, at least fulfilment of a sort.

Although I was over twenty, and had been earning my own living for over three years, in many ways I was still a boy, with a boy's thoughts and dreams—dreams of romance, high adventure and good companionship. And I was still a lonely boy, alone on that big ship—passengers and crew all strangers to me—sailing into an uncertain future.

I had two books with me—Thoreau's *Walden* and Richard Jefferies' *The Story of My Heart*—both reflecting my burgeoning interest in the natural world—but during the day the cabin was hot and stuffy, and the decks, too crowded, so I postponed most of my reading until the journey was over. But at night, when it was cool on the deck, and most of the passengers were down below, watching a film or drinking Polish vodka (the Batory was a Polish ship), I would sit out under the stars while the ship ploughed on through the Red Sea, bringing me home to India. There was no sound but the dull thunder of the ship's screws and the faint tinkle of music from an open porthole.

And as I sat there, pondering over my future, a line from Thoreau kept running through my head. 'Lonely! Why should I feel lonely? Is not our planet in the Milky Way?'

Wherever I went, the stars were there to keep me company. And I knew that as long as I connected, in both a physical and mystical way, with the natural world—sea, sun, earth, moon and stars—I would never feel lonely upon this planet.

SKY ABOVE THE MOUNTAINS

A night in the mountains:
It is the beginning of summer and I have trekked with a friend to his village in the Garhwal Himalayas. It has taken us a full day, and we are greeted outside the village by a buffalo herd wending its way homeward in the twilight, the gurgle of hookahs and the homely smell of cow-dung smoke.

And after an evening with friends over rum, and a partridge for dinner, we retire to our beds: I to my charpai under a lime tree at the edge of the courtyard. The moon had not yet risen and the cicadas are silent.

I stretch myself out on the charpai under a sky tremendous with stars. And as I close my eyes someone brushes against the lime tree, bruising its leaves, and the good fresh fragrance of lime comes to me on the night air, making the moment memorable for all time.

◆

A morning in the mountains:

I wake to the sound of a loud cicada in the lime tree near my bed. It is just after first light, and through the pattern of the leaves I see the outlines of the mighty Himalayas as they stride away into an immensity of sky. I can see the small house, where I am a guest, standing in the middle of its narrow terraced fields. I can see the other houses, standing a little apart from each other in their own bits of land. I can see trees and bushes, and a path leading up the hill to the deodar forest on the summit.

The tops of the distant mountains suddenly light up as the sun torches the snow peaks. A door bangs open. The house is stirring. A cock belatedly welcomes the daylight and elsewhere in the village dogs are barking. A magpie flies with a whirring sound as it crosses the courtyard and then glides downhill. And suddenly everyone, everything comes to life, and the village is buzzing with activity.

◆

Trekking in the Himalayan foothills back when I could do that, I once walked for kilometres without encountering habitation. I was just scolding myself for not having brought along a water bottle when I came across a patch of green on a rock face. I parted a curtain of tender maidenhair fern and discovered a tiny spring issuing from the rock—nectar for the thirsty traveller.

I stayed there for hours, watching the water descend, drop by drop, into a tiny casement in the rocks. Each drop reflected creation. That same spring, I later discovered, joined other springs to form a swift, tumbling stream, which went cascading down the hill into other streams until, in the plains, it became part of a river. And that river flowed into another mightier river that kilometres later emptied into the ocean.

Be like water, taught Lao-Tzu, philosopher and founder

of Taoism. Soft and limpid, it finds its way through, over or under any obstacle, sometimes travelling underground for great distances before emerging into the open. It does not quarrel; it simply moves on.

SO BEAUTIFUL THE NIGHT

I love the night, Lord.
After the sun's heat and the day's work,
it's good to close my eyes and rest my body.
It's a good time for small creatures:
Porcupines come out of their burrows
to dig for roots.
The night-jar calls tonk-tonk!
The timid owl peeps out of his hole in the tree trunk
Where he has been hiding all day.
Insects crawl out in thousands.
The wind comes down the chimney
and blows around the room.
I'm watching the stars from my window.
The trees are stretching their arms in the dark
and whispering to the moon.
But if the trees could walk, Lord,
What a wonderful sight it would be—
Armies of pines and firs and oaks
Marching over the moonlit mountains.

MATHURA'S HALLOWED HAUNTS

Mathura, most sacred of cities, stands on the right bank of the Yamuna northwest of Agra. All men speak of Mathura with reverence, and it has been said that 'if a man spend in Banaras all his lifetime, he has earned less merit than if he passes but a single day in the sacred city of Mathura.'

It is difficult to pierce the fog which hides the date of the city's birth; but sacred it has always been, as the capital of the kingdom of Braj and the birthplace of Lord Krishna: 'Teacher and Soul of the Universe. Destroyer of the earth's tyrant kings, and the First of the Spirits...'

I went to Mathura at the end of the rains. The fields and the trees were alive with strange, beautiful birds: the long-tailed king crow; innumerable doves in shades of blue and green; kingfishers and bluejays and weaver-birds; and, resting on a telegraph pole, the great white-headed kite, which, some say, was Garuda, Vishnu's famous steed. Resplendent, too, were the green and gold parrots, from among whom Kamadeva, the god of love, chose his steed. Armed with his sugarcane bow with its string made of bees,

Kamadeva still rides at night over the plains of Mathura. Many are the journeys he makes on nights approaching the full moon. He knows the ways of men and women, and his bow, like Cupid's, is always ready to assist the ardent lover.

In the tanks and 'jheels' around Mathura I saw a variety of game birds—wild duck, herbits, cranes and snipe—but all life is sacred for many miles around Mathura, and not even the bird trapper is permitted to lay his snares.

Strutting under an old tamarind tree are Krishna's birds, the brilliant peacocks. Centuries ago, they gave the city their name, and today Mathura is still known as the Peacock City. The peacocks seem to know that they are the chosen of Krishna. Spreading out their many-hued fantails, they glance at us drab mortals with an air of disdain.

Near Mathura is Brindavan in whose forests—they have gone now—the boy Krishna and his brother Balram ran wild, playing on their shepherds' pipes. The neighbours found Krishna very mischievous. He was extremely fond of butter and, going by stealth one day to the house of a neighbour, climbed onto a shelf to get at a large jar of butter. He ate the butter as far as he could reach, and then got into the jar. The owner, on returning, found him there and putting a cover on the jar to prevent the boy from escaping went to Krishna's father to make a complaint. But when he arrived at the house it was not the father who met him but the little butter-thief.

There is another story which tells us of the day Krishna stole his mother's curds, and finished them while no one was looking. 'O, you wicked one!' exclaimed his mother when she discovered what had happened. 'Come, let me see your mouth.' And when she looked into his mouth, she saw the Universe—the earth, sea and heavens; the sun and the moon, the planets and all the stars…

Brindavan stands on a tongue of land surrounded by the river, which has curved here in a strange fashion. Legend tells us that Balram, who was very strong, once led a dance on the Yamuna's bank, but moved his giant limbs so clumsily that the river laughed aloud and taunted him, saying: 'Enough, my clumsy child! How can you hope to dance as Krishna, who is divine?' Balram was very angry with the river, and taking his great plough he traced a furrow from the brink of the river; but so deep was the furrow that the river fell into it and was led far astray.

When the tyrant king Kamsa heard of the unusual exploits of Krishna and Balram, he planned to have them killed in case they became a danger to his power. He sent a message to the brothers, inviting them to a contest of arms in the royal city of Mathura. Krishna and Balram accepted the challenge.

On the day of the contest, King Kamsa sat on a lofty throne near the arena. As Krishna and Balram entered, a mighty elephant was sent against them. But Krishna, seizing the animal by the tail, swung it around his head and threw it to the ground. Then each of the brothers taking a tusk, they slew Kamsa's mightiest champions. Kamsa ordered his army to kill the boys, but Krishna sprang up the steps of the throne, seized the king by his hair and hurled him into a deep ravine.

Visitors to Mathura are still shown the mound where Kamsa's throne once stood. And still venerated is that part of the riverfront where the two boys rested after dragging the body of Kamsa down to the funeral pyre.

I wandered in the streets of the city past shops gleaming with brasswork or piled high with pedas, Mathura's famous sweets. From the bridge, I could see the riverfront with its innumerable temples. And below, hundreds of majestic tortoises watched the bathers and the boatmen with speculative eyes. Sometimes a boatman seized one of these longnecked creatures and held it up to view. The tortoise would immediately draw its legs into its shell—a vivid illustration of the theory that nothing is annihilated but only disappears, the effect being absorbed in the cause!

JAIPUR

As we still had a few days left of our holiday, and a little money, and as neither Kamal nor I was anxious to return to Delhi earlier than was necessary, we decided to sneak off to Jaipur for a day or two. We had both been to Jaipur before, but it is a city that one can visit again and again without ever tiring of its charm.

There is an atmosphere about Jaipur—once the most beautiful city in India, and one of the earliest planned cities in the world which even to the casual visitor distinguishes it from other towns. This is probably due to the almost entire absence of any European or Western influence in the architecture and planning of the town.

Founded in 1728 by the brilliant astronomer-king Maharaja Jai Singh II, it is quite unlike any other town in India or Asia: no tortuous gloomy streets or squalid overcrowded bazaars. Its six main streets are very wide and straight, one running the whole length of the town, the others crossing it at right angles, dividing the city into rectangular blocks. These are enclosed by a high wall, its parapets loopholed for musketry, into which are set seven entrance gates.

On the northwest side the hills rise sheer beyond the city, bearing on their summit the Nahargarh or Tiger Fort. Not needed now for purposes of war, it houses much of the wealth of this former states ruler. Guarded not by troops but by men of the robber caste, this wealth lay hoarded for centuries, potential but never used capital, typical of the ways of the East.

In the city itself, narrow streets are found in plenty, for a network of them connects the wide main roads. So narrow are some, that the bougainvillea sprawls from the upper storey of one building to its opposite across the way. But curiously enough, they are nearly all straight, and a passing glimpse from the main street reveals their whole length. Sometimes these lanes are full of little shops, but many of them contain only private houses, where occasionally a half-open door reveals a glimpse of the grass and fountain of a garden or courtyard beyond.

The great attraction of the main streets is their spaciousness and the beautiful facade of the tall buildings which line them, most colour-washed in a dull, pale old-rose tone, some showing the soft amber or grey of the original limestone. In some of them the plain walls are varied with beautiful little chhattris, while here and there the old carved domes of some Jain temple break the flat line of roofs.

The street walls of these houses—which are really only the walls of the outer courtyard, the main building being behind and cut off from the street altogether—can boast of only the smallest windows, for these were meant to conceal, and not reveal, the zenana quarters behind. The quaint figures of elephants and other animals painted on the walls give them the appearance of dolls' houses when seen from the road below, though many of them are three or four storeys in height and from a distance look very imposing.

The streets themselves are a feast of colour and interest. Every mode of progression can be seen here, from ambling bullock carts and ekkas, with their quaintly shaped and brightly coloured hoods, to buses and streamlined motor cars. There are strings of camels bearing fodder, and elephants that amble up the road to the Amber Palace, and here and there wanders the ubiquitous Brahmani bull. All along the streets and around the squares throng hundreds of pigeons—sacred birds throughout Rajasthan—being fed by the passers-by or helping themselves to food on the stalls.

All along the ground floor of the buildings, and cut off from them by a small projecting tin roof along which the langurs run up and down in play, are the bazaar shops, little hives of industry doing a brisk trade. Busier still are the wide pavements in front; they are chock-a-block with stalls and with groups of artisans plying their trade in the midst of the passers-by.

We saw great piles of yellow maize and corn, of jawar and bajra, heaped upon the pavement, while to one side people were busy making the grain on primitive grindstones, laughing and singing as they ceaselessly wound the handle, three of them often working at one grinder. A little further on, what seemed at a distance to be a rich Herati rug flung down resolved itself into masses of chillies spread for yards along the pavement to dry in the sun. Then came the vegetables and fruit piled high in baskets, the countrywomen who had brought them squatting in the midst, sorting and selling and often nursing their babies at the same time.

Next came a little colony of brass workers sitting at the pavement's edge, engraving patterns on brass trays, plates and vessels, and then inlaying them with sticks of coloured enamel. Unlike them, the dyers generally work within their shops. In one of these we saw a whole family variously employed, from the old grandfather, who was mixing brilliant dyes in great brass cauldrons, to the latest infant, sitting in the middle and watching the others with an open mouth, while the family goat and attendant kid ambled in and out at will. Two of the family, a pugree-length of gaudy cloth just freshly dyed between them, walked up and down the pavement, waving it in the air to dry. The street had the appearance of being hung with bunting.

Most amusing of all, we came suddenly on three rows of little boys standing on the pavement with their slates at their feet. To one side stood the enterprising schoolmaster, while in front a small urchin with head craned forward loudly chanted the words of some lesson, which the class, in a medley of hoarse and squeaky voices, repeated after him. The intense concentration of this determined little group seemed in no way upset by the surrounding bustle and confusion.

There are few palaces in India to surpass the grandeur of the famous old palace of Amber. It lies northwest of the city, approached by a narrow pass in the hills which shuts off all view of Jaipur and opens on a little valley almost entirely closed by hills. Above a small lake, built on the barren hillside, stand the still perfect walls of this majestic fortress-palace. Their limestone blocks are mellowed to a soft amber colour, and the marble is now a rich cream.

The palace, now deserted except for its temple to the goddess Kali, is still in perfect condition. Its sun-soaked courtyards are open to the sky, and its empty pillared halls are full of echoes.

THE FURTHER ONE GOES

In the good old, bad old days, before the First World War, no one bothered about passports and immigration procedures. The hazards of travel were disincentives in themselves. But now that travel has become swift, comfortable and relatively painless, new obstacles arise in the form of travel documents, income-tax and health certificates, foreign exchange regulations and other diabolical trappings of the twentieth century.

We need concern ourselves no longer about the reliability of camels or the safety of canoes, the seaworthiness of sailing-ships or the hazards of the stagecoach. But, there is the slight possibility of our plane being hijacked, or of crashing into the sea and saving our relatives the cost of a funeral. (Even so, one can have the satisfaction of plunging to ones doom strapped into a well-padded seat, with a glass of Scotch clutched in one's trembling hand, while someone makes an announcement that everything is under control. Our forefathers died the hard way.)

Travel, it used to be said, broadened the mind. I'm not certain that it ever did, but it certainly doesn't do so any more.

Undoubtedly it broadens the bottom. Most of the time—in plane, airport lounge, all-night bar or luxury coach—one is sitting for long periods on one's fanny; and if you sit on anything for a long time it is liable to get broader. But I doubt if one learns much about the rest of the world from hotels and airports.

Modern travel is obviously designed for people in a hurry. One international airline acknowledges, in a glossy ad in a foreign magazine, that a business trip halfway around the world can be the 'most hectic part of your hectic life,' and undertakes to make it as relaxed and enjoyable as the hectic circumstances permit. In this crowded shrinking, hurrying world, even relaxation is something that has to be taken at the gallop.

There are no quiet corners left for quiet people; no undiscovered lands for explorers; no unmapped territories for adventurers; no lonely stretches of beach, no mysterious hidden rivers... Romance died with Lord Jim.

Still, if it's a hectically relaxed business trip that you want, then by all means travel. But if it's your mind that you intend broadening, you would do better to stay at home and tend your orchids or geraniums. Nero Wolfe, Rex Stout's great armchair detective, was convinced that, in nine cases out of ten, the places that people go to are no improvement upon the places that they come from.

Lao Tzu, who lived in the sixth century BC, was even more succinct. 'The further one goes,' he said, 'the less one knows.'

PICNIC AT FOX BURN

In spite of the frenetic building activity in most hill-stations, there are still a few ruins to be found on the outskirts— neglected old bungalows that have fallen or been pulled down, and which now provide shelter for bats, owls, stray goats, itinerant sadhus and sometimes the restless spirits of those who once dwelt in them.

One such ruin is Fox-Burn, but I won't tell you exactly where it can be found, because I visit the place for purposes of meditation (or just plain contemplation) and I would hate to arrive there one morning to find about fifty people picnicking on the grass.

And yet it did witness a picnic of sorts the other day, when the children accompanied me to the ruin. They had heard it was haunted, and they wanted to see the ghost.

Rakesh is twelve, Mukesh is six, and Dolly is four, and they are not afraid of ghosts.

I should mention here, that before Fox-Burn became a ruin, back in the 1940s, it was owned by an elderly English woman,

Mrs Williams, who ran it as a boarding-house for several years. In the end, poor health forced her to give up this work, and during her last years, she lived alone in the huge house, with just a chowkidar to help. Her children, who had grown up on the property, had long since settled in faraway lands.

When Mrs Williams died, the chowkidar stayed on for some time until the property was disposed of; but he left as soon as he could. Late at night there would be a loud rapping on his door, and he would hear the old lady calling out: 'Shamsher Singh, open the door! Open the door, I say, and let me in!'

Needless to say, Shamsher Singh kept the door firmly closed. He returned to his village at the first opportunity. The hill-station was going through a slump at the time, and the new owners pulled the house down and sold the roof and beams as scrap.

'What does Fox-Burn mean?' asked Rakesh, as we climbed the neglected, overgrown path to the ruin.

'Well, Burn is a Scottish word meaning stream or spring. Perhaps there was a spring here, once. If so, it dried up long ago.'

'And did a fox live here?'

'Maybe a fox came to drink at the spring. There are still foxes living on the mountain. Sometimes you can see them dancing in the moonlight.'

Passing through a gap in a wall, we came upon the ruins of the house. In the bright light of a summer morning it did not look in the least spooky or depressing. A line of Doric pillars were all that remained of what must have been an elegant porch and verandah. Beyond them, through the deodars, we could see the distant snows. It must have been a lovely spot in which to spend the better part of one's life. No wonder Mrs Williams wanted to come back.

The children were soon scampering about on the grass,

whilst I sought shelter beneath a huge chestnut tree.

There is no tree so friendly as the chestnut, especially in summer when it is in full leaf.

Mukesh discovered an empty water-tank and Rakesh suggested that it had once fed the burn that no longer existed. Dolly busied herself making nosegays with the daisies that grew wild in the grass.

Rakesh looked up suddenly. He pointed to a path on the other side of the ruin, and exclaimed: 'Look, what's that? Is it Mrs Williams?'

'A ghost!' said Mukesh excitedly.

But it turned out to be the local washerwoman, a large white bundle on her head, taking a short-cut across the property.

A more peaceful place could hardly be imagined, until a large black dog, a spaniel of sorts, arrived on the scene. He wanted someone to play with—indeed, he insisted on playing—and ran circles round us until we threw sticks for him to fetch and gave him half our sandwiches.

'Whose dog is it?' asked Rakesh.

'I've no idea.'

'Did Mrs Williams keep a black dog?'

'Is it a ghost dog?' asked Mukesh.

'It looks real to me,' I said.

'And it's eaten all my biscuits,' said Dolly.

'Don't ghosts have to eat?' asked Mukesh.

'I don't know. We'll have to ask one.'

'It can't be any fun being a ghost if you can't eat,' declared Mukesh.

The black dog left us as suddenly as he had appeared, and as there was no sign of an owner, I began to wonder if he had not, after all, been an apparition.

A cloud came over the sun, the air grew chilly.

'Let's go home,' said Mukesh.

'I'm hungry,' said Rakesh.

'Come along, Dolly,' I called.

But Dolly couldn't be seen.

We called out to her, and looked behind trees and pillars, certain that she was hiding from us. Almost five minutes passed in searching for her, and a sick feeling of apprehension was coming over me, when Dolly emerged from the ruins and ran towards us.

'Where have you been?' we demanded, almost with one voice.

'I was playing—in there—in the old house. Hide and seek.'

'On your own?'

'No, there were two children. A boy and a girl. They were playing too.'

'I haven't seen any children,' I said.

'They've gone now.'

'Well, it's time we went too.'

We set off down the winding path, with Rakesh leading the way, and then we had to wait because Dolly had stopped and was waving to someone.

'Who are you waving to, Dolly?'

'To the children.'

'Where are they?'

'Under the chestnut tree.'

'I can't see them. Can you see them, Rakesh? Can you, Mukesh?'

Rakesh and Mukesh said they couldn't see any children. But Dolly was still waving.

'Goodbye,' she called. 'Goodbye!'

Were there voices on the wind? Faint voices calling goodbye? Could Dolly see something we couldn't see?

'We can't see anyone,' I said.

'No,' said Dolly. 'But they can see me!'

Then she left off her game and joined us, and we ran home laughing. Mrs Williams may not have revisited her old house that day but perhaps her children had been there, playing under the chestnut tree they had known so long ago.

THE TAJ AT HIGH NOON

It is high noon on a summer's day in Agra, and I am the only visitor at the Taj.

'You should see the Taj by moonlight,' everyone tells me; but these are dark nights, and anyway, I have to be in Delhi in a few hours. Instead of lingering and loafing as I am usually given to doing, I find myself chained, like a package-tour tourist, to a time-schedule. I have only one hour to spend at the magnificent mausoleum built by an emperor to preserve the memory of a cherished wife. And so, like mad dogs and Englishman, I go out in the mid-day sun.

It is difficult to view the Taj at high noon. The fierce sun strikes the white marble, and there is a great dazzle of reflected light. One stands there with averted eyes, looking at everything—the formal gardens, the surrounding walls of red sandstone, the scene across the river—everything except the monument one has come to see.

It is there, of course, very solid and real, perfectly preserved, with every jade, jasper or lapis-lazuli stone embedded in its rightful place; and after a while one can shade one's eyes and take in a vision of shimmering white marble. The heat rises in waves from the pavement, and the squares of black and white marble create an effect of running water. Inside the chamber it is cool and dark and, after a while, rather musty—so much so that one hurries up again into the blazing sunlight.

I walk the length of a gallery and turn with some relief to the river scene. The sluggish Jamuna winds past Agra on its way to union with the Ganga. I know the Jamuna well. I know where it emerges from the foothills, cold and blue from the melting snows; I know it as it winds through fields of wheat and mustard and sugar cane, across the flat plains of Uttar Pradesh sometimes placid, sometimes in flood. I know the river at Delhi, where its muddy banks are a patchwork of clothes spread out by the hundreds of washermen who serve the city.

And I know it at Mathura, where it is alive with huge turtles. Mathura, sacred city, whose beginnings are lost in antiquity; birthplace of Lord Krishna, whose every exploit is linked with the riverside ghats, forests and temples. And then the river wends its way through Agra, to this spot by the Taj, where parrots flash in the sunshine, and kingfishers swoop low over the water, and a proud peacock struts across the grass that carpets the approach to the monument.

I followed the peacock into a shady grove. It is quite tame and does not fly away. It leads me to a small boy who is sitting in the shade of a tree feasting on a handful of some small green fruit.

I have not seen this fruit before; I ask the boy what it is. He offers me what looks like a hard green plum.

'It is called Kamrak,' says the boy. 'There are many Kamrak

trees in the garden.'

'Are you allowed to pick the fruit?' I ask.

'I am allowed,' he says, flashing me a smile. 'My father is the head gardener!'

I bite into the fruit. It is hard and sour, but not unpleasant. 'Do you live here?' I ask.

'On the other side of the wall,' he says. 'But I come here every day, to help my father—and to eat the fruit.'

'So you see the Taj Mahal every day?'

'I have seen it every day for as long as I can remember.'

'And I am seeing it today only... You are very lucky!'

He shrugs. 'If you see it once, or a hundred times, it is the same thing. It doesn't change.'

'Don't you like looking at the Taj?'

'I like looking at the people who come here. They are always different. In the evenings, when it is cool, there are many people.'

'You must have seen people from almost every country in the world.'

'That is true. They all come here to look at the Taj. And I look at them. In that way, it isn't boring.'

'Well, you have the Taj to thank for that.'

He looks thoughtfully at the shimmering monument. His eyes are accustomed to the fierce sun; but it seems as though he is looking at the Taj for the first time. He sees it every day but at this moment he is really looking at it. He is thinking about it, wondering what magic it must possess to attract people from all corners of the earth, to bring them here walking through his father's well-kept garden so that he can have something new and fresh to look at each day.

And as he looks, a cloud—a very small cloud—passes across the face of the sun; and in the softened light I am able to look at the Taj without screwing up my eyes and I see it in all its splendour.

As the boy said, it doesn't change. Therein lies its beauty. For the effect on the traveller is the same today as it was three hundred years ago when the Frenchman, Bernier, wrote: 'Nothing offends the eye... No part can be found that is not skillfully wrought, or that has not its peculiar beauty.'

And so, for a few moments, this poem in marble is on view for two people—the traveller and the gardener's boy.

We say nothing; there is nothing to be said.

But now, many months later, when I try to recapture the essence of that day, it is not the monument itself that I remember most vividly. The Taj is there, of course: I still see it as a mirror for the sun. But what remains with me more than anything else is the passage of the river and the sharp flavour of the Kamrak fruit.

ROAD TO BADRINATH

If you have travelled up the Mandakini valley, and then cross over into the valley of the Alaknanda, you are immediately struck by the contrast. The Mandakini is gentler, richer in vegetation, almost pastoral in places; the Alaknanda is awesome, precipitous, threatening and seemingly inhospitable to those who must live and earn a livelihood in its confines.

Even as we left Chamoli and began the steady, winding climb to Badrinath, the nature of the terrain underwent a dramatic change. No longer did green fields slope gently down to the riverbed. Here they clung precariously to rocky slopes and ledges that grew steeper and narrower, while the river below, impatient to reach its confluence with the Bhagirathi at Deoprayag, thundered along a narrow gorge.

Badrinath is one of the four Dhams, or four most holy places in India (the other three are Rameshwaram, Dwarka and Jagannath Puri). For the pilgrim travelling to his holiest of holies, the journey is exciting, possibly even uplifting; but for those who live permanently on these crags and ridges, life is harsh, a struggle from one day to the next. No wonder so many young men from Garhwal make their way into the Army. Little grows on these rocky promontories; and what does is at the mercy of the weather. For most of the year the fields lie fallow. Rivers, unfortunately, run downhill and not uphill.

The harshness of this life, typical of much of Garhwal, was brought home to me at Pipalkoti, where we stopped for the night. Pilgrims stop here by the coachload, for the Garhwal Mandal Vikas Nigam's rest house is fairly capacious and small hotels and dharamsalas abound. Just off the busy road is a tiny hospital, and here, late in the evening, we came across a woman keeping vigil over the dead body of her husband. The body had been laid out on a bench in the courtyard. A few feet away the road was crowded with pilgrims in festival mood; no one glanced over the low wall to notice this tragic scene.

The woman came from a village near Helong. Earlier that day, finding her consumptive husband in a critical condition, she had decided to bring him to the nearest town for treatment. As he was frail and emaciated, she was able to carry him on her back for several miles until she reached the motor road. Then, at some expense, she engaged a passing taxi and brought him to Pipalkoti. But he was already dead when she reached the small hospital. There was no morgue; so she sat beside the body in the courtyard, waiting for dawn and the arrival of others from the village. A few men arrived next morning, and we saw them wending their way down to the cremation ground. We did not see the woman again. Her children were hungry and she had to hurry home to look after them.

Pipalkoti is hot (and pipal trees are conspicuous by their absence), but Joshimath, the winter resort of the Badrinath temple establishment, is about 6,000 ft above sea level and has an equable climate. It is now a fairly large town, and although the surrounding hills are rather bare, it does have one great tree that has survived the ravages of time. This is an ancient mulberry, known as the Kalpa-Vriksha (Immortal Wishing Tree), beneath which the great Sankaracharya meditated a few centuries ago. It is reputedly over two thousand years old, and is certainly larger than my modest four-roomed flat in Mussoorie. Sixty pilgrims holding hands might just about encircle its trunk.

I have seen some big trees, but this is certainly the oldest and broadest of them. I am glad that Sankaracharya meditated beneath it and thus ensured its preservation. Otherwise it might well have gone the way of other great trees and forests that once flourished in this area.

A small boy reminds me that it is a Wishing Tree, so I make my wish. I wish that other trees might prosper like this.

'Have you made a wish?' I ask the boy.

'I wish that you will give me one rupee,' he says.

His wish comes true with immediate effect. Mine lies in an uncertain future. But he has given me a lesson in wishing.

Joshimath has to be a fairly large place because most of Badrinath arrives here in November, when the shrine is snowbound for six months. Army and PWD structures also dot the landscape. This is no carefree hill resort, but it has all the amenities for making a short stay quite pleasant and interesting. Perched on the steep mountainside above the junction of the Alaknanda and Dhauli rivers, it is now vastly different from what it was when Frank Smythe visited it fifty years ago and described it as 'an ugly little place…straggling unbeautifully over the hillside'. Primitive little shops line the main street, which is roughly paved in places and in others has been deeply channelled by the monsoon rains. The pilgrims spend the night in single-storeyed rest houses, not unlike the hovels provided for the Kentish hop-pickers of former days, and are filthy and evil-smelling'.

Those were Joshimath's former days. It is a different place today, with small hotels, modern shops, a cinema and its growth and comparative modernity dates from the early sixties when the old pilgrim footpath gave way to the motor road which takes the traveller all the way to Badrinath. No longer does the weary, footsore pilgrim sink gratefully down in the shade of the Kalpa-Vriksha. He alights from his bus or luxury coach and drinks a Cola or a Thums-up at one of the many small restaurants on the roadside.

Contrast this comfortable journey with the pilgrimage fifty years ago. Frank Smythe again: 'So they venture on their pilgrimage... Some borne magnificently by coolies, some toiling along in rags, some almost crawling, preyed on by disease and distorted by dreadful deformities... Europeans who have read and travelled cannot conceive what goes on in the minds of these simple folk, many of them from the agricultural parts of India. Wonderment and fear must be the prime ingredients. So the pilgrimage becomes an adventure. Unknown dangers threaten the broad well-made path, at any moment the Gods, who hold the rocks in leash, may unloose their wrath upon the hapless passerby. To the European it is a walk to Badrinath, to the Hindu pilgrim it is far, far more.'

Above Vishnuprayag, Smythe left the Alaknanda and entered the Bhyundar valley, a botanist's paradise, which he called the Valley of Flowers. He fell in love with the lush meadows of this high valley and made it known to the world. It continues to attract the botanist and trekker. Primulas of subtle shades, wild geraniums, saxifrages clinging to the rocks, yellow and red potentillas, snow-white anemones, delphiniums, violets, wild roses, all these and many more flourish there, capturing the mind and heart of the flower-lover.

'Impossible to take a step without crushing a flower.' This may not be true any more, for many footsteps have trodden the Bhyundar in recent years. There are other areas in Garhwal where the hills are rich in flora—the Har-ki-Doon, Harsil, Tungnath, and the Khiraun valley where the Balsam grows to a height of eight feet—but the Bhyundar has both a variety and a concentration of wild flowers, especially towards the end of the monsoon. It would be no exaggeration to call it one of the most beautiful valleys in the world.

The Bhyundar is a digression for lovers of mountain scenery; but the pilgrim keeps his eyes fixed on the ultimate goal— Badrinath, where the gods dwell and where salvation is to be found.

There are still a few who do it the hard way—mostly those who have taken sanyas and renounced the world. Here is one hardy soul doing penance. He stretches himself out on the ground, draws himself up to a standing position, then flattens himself out again. In this manner he will proceed from Badrinath to Rishikesh, oblivious of the sun and rain, the dust from passing buses, the sharp gravel of the footpath.

Others are not so hardy. One saffron-robed scholar speaking fair English asks us for a lift to Badrinath, and we find a space for him. He rewards us with a long and involved commentary on the vedas, which lasts through the remainder of the journey. His special field of study, he informs us, is the part played by aeronautics in Vedic literature.

'And what,' I ask him, 'is the connection between the two?'

He looks at me pityingly.

'It is what I am trying to find out,' he replies.

The road drops to Pandukeshwar and rises again, and all the time I am scanning the horizon for the forests of the Badrinath region I had read about many years ago in Eraser's *Himalaya Mountains*. Walnuts growing up to 9,000 ft, deodars and Bilka up to 9,500 ft, and Amesh and Kiusu fir to a similar height—but, apart from strands of long-leaved and excelsia pine, I do not see much, certainly no deodars. What has happened to them, I wonder. An endless variety of trees delighted us all the way from Dugalbeta to Mandal, a well-protected area, but here on the high ridges above the Alaknanda, little seems to grow: or, if ever anything did, it has long since been bespoiled or swept away.

Finally we reach the windswept, barren valley which harbours Badrinath—a growing township, thriving, lively, but somewhat dwarfed by the snow-capped peaks that tower above it. As at Joshimath, there is no dearth of hostelries and dharamsalas. Even so, every hotel or rest house is overcrowded. It is the height of the pilgrim season, and pilgrims, tourists and mendicants of every description throng the river front.

Just as Kedar is the most sacred of the Shiva temples in the Himalayas, similarly Badrinath is the supreme place of worship for the Vaishnav sects.

According to legend, when Sankaracharya in his Digvijaya travels visited the Mana valley, he arrived at the Narada-Kund and found fifty different images lying in its waters. These he rescued, and when he had done so, a voice from Heaven said: 'These are the images for the Kaliyug, establish them here.' Sankaracharya accordingly placed them beneath a mighty tree which grew there and whose shade extended from Badrinath to Nandprayag, a distance of over eighty miles. Close to it was the hermitage of Nar-Nandprayag (or Arjuna and Krishna), and in course of time temples were built in honour of these and other manifestations of Vishnu. It was here that Vishnu appeared to his followers in person, as four-armed, crested and adorned with pearls and garlands. The faithful, it is said, can still see him on the peak of Nilkantha, on the great Kumbha day. It is in fact the Nilkantha peak that dominates this crater-like valley, where a few hardy thistles and nettles manage to survive. Like cacti in the desert, the pricklier forms of life seem best equipped to live in a hostile environment.

Nilkantha means blue-necked, an allusion to Lord Shiva's swallowing of a poison meant to destroy the world. The poison remained in his throat, which was rendered blue thereafter. It is a majestic and awe-inspiring peak, soaring to a height of 21,640 ft. As its summit is only five miles from Badrinath, it is justly held in reverence. From its ice-clad pinnacle, three great ridges sweep down, of which the south terminates in the Alaknanda valley.

On the evening of our arrival we could not see the peak, as it was hidden in cloud. Badrinath itself was shrouded in mist. But we made our way to the temple, a gaily decorated building, about fifty feet high, with a gilded roof. The image of Vishnu, carved in black stone, stands in the centre of the sanctum, opposite the door, in a Dhyana posture. An endless stream of people pass through the temple to pay homage and emerge the better for their proximity to the divine.

From the temple, flights of steps lead down to the rushing river and to the hot springs which emerge just above it. Another road leads through a long but tidy bazaar where pilgrims may buy mementos of their visit—from sacred amulets to pictures of the gods in vibrant technicolour. Here at last I am free to indulge my passion for cheap rings, with none to laugh at my foible. There are all kinds, from rings designed like a coiled serpent (my favourite) to twisted bands of copper and iron and others containing the pictures of gods, gurus and godmen. They do not cost more than two or three rupees each, and so I am able to fill my pockets. I never wear these rings. I simply hoard them away. My friends are convinced that in a previous existence I was a jackdaw, seizing upon and hiding away any kind of bright and shiny object!

India is a land of crowds, and it is no different at Badrinath where people throng together, all in good spirits. Hindus enjoy their religion. Whether bathing in cold streams or hot springs, or tramping from one sacred mountain shrine to another, they are united in their wish to experience something of the magic and mystique of the gods and glories of another epoch.

Even those who have renounced the world appear to be cheerful—like the young woman from Gujarat who had taken sanyas, and who met me on the steps below the temple. She gave me a dazzling smile and passed me an exercise book. She had taken a vow of silence; but being, I think, of an extrovert nature, she seemed eager to remain in close communication with the rest of humanity, and did so by means of written questions and answers. Hence the exercise book. Together we filled three pages of it before she told me that she wished to proceed on pilgrimage to Amarnath but was short of funds. With help from my generous companion, we made her a donation, and with a flashing smile of thanks she left us and was lost in the crowd.

Although at Badrinath I missed the sound of birds and the presence of trees, there were other compensations. It was good to be part of the happy throng at its colourful little temple and to see the sacred river close to its source. And early next morning I was rewarded with the loveliest experience of all.

Opening the window of my room and glancing out, I saw the rising sun touch the snow-clad summit of Nilkantha. At first the snows were pink; then they turned to orange and gold. All sleep vanished as I gazed up in wonder at that magnificent pinnacle in the sky. And had Lord Vishnu appeared just then on the summit, I would not have been in the least surprised.

AT THE END OF THE ROAD

Choose your companions carefully when you are walking in
the hills. If you are accompanied by the wrong person—by
which I mean someone who is temperamentally very different
to you—that long hike you've been dreaming of could well
turn into a nightmare.

This has happened to me more than once. The first time,
many years ago, when I accompanied a businessman-friend to
the Pindari Glacier in Kumaon. He was in such a hurry to
get back to his executive's desk in Delhi that he set off for the
Glacier as though he had a train to catch, refusing to spend
any time admiring the views, looking for birds or animals, or
greeting the local inhabitants. By the time we had left the last
dak bungalow at Phurkia, I was ready to push him over a cliff.
He probably felt the same way about me.

On our way down, we met a party of Delhi University boys
who were on the same trek. They were doing it in a leisurely,
good-humoured fashion. They were very friendly and asked me
to join them. On an impulse, I bid farewell to my previous

companion—who was only too glad to dash off downhill to where his car was parked at Kapkote—while I made a second ascent to the Glacier, this time in better company.

Unfortunately, my previous companion had been the one with the funds. My new friends fed me on the way back, and in Nainital I pawned my watch so that I could have enough for the bus ride back to Delhi. Lesson Two: always carry enough money with you; don't depend on a wealthy friend!

Of course, it's hard to know who will be a 'good companion' until you have actually hit the road together. Sharing a meal or having a couple of drinks together is not the same as tramping along on a dusty road with the water bottle down to its last drop. You can't tell until you have spent a night in the rain, or lost the way in the mountains, or finished all the food, whether both of you have stout hearts and a readiness for the unknown.

I like walking alone, but a good companion is well worth finding. He will add to the experience. 'Give me a companion of my way, be it only to mention how the shadows lengthen as the sun declines,' wrote Hazlitt.

Pratap was one such companion. He had invited me to spend a fortnight with him in his village above the Nayar river in Pauri-Garhwal. In those days, there was no motor-road beyond Lansdowne and one had to walk some thirty miles to get to the village.

But first, one had to get to Lansdowne. This involved getting into a train at Dehra Dun, getting out at Luxor (across the Ganga), getting into another train, and then getting out again at Najibabad and waiting for a bus to take one through the Tarai to Kotdwara.

Najibabad must have been one of the least inspiring places on earth. Hot, dusty, apparently lifeless. We spent two hours at the bus-stand, in the company of several donkeys, also quartered there. We were told that the area had once been the favourite hunting ground of a notorious dacoit, Sultana Daku, whose fortress overlooked the barren plain. I could understand him taking up dacoity—what else was there to do in such a place—and presumed that he looked elsewhere for his loot, for in Nazibabad there was nothing worth taking. In due course he was betrayed and hanged by the British, when they should instead have given him an OBE for stirring up the sleepy countryside.

There was a short branch line from Nazibabad to Kotdwara, but the train wasn't leaving that day, as the engine driver was unaccountably missing. The bus driver seemed to be missing too, but he did eventually turn up, a little worse for some late night drinking. I could sympathize with him. If in 1940, Nazibabad drove you to dacoity, in 1960 it drove you to drink.

Kotdwara, a steamy little town in the foothills, was equally depressing. It seemed to lack any sort of character. Here we changed buses, and moved into higher regions, and the higher we went, the nicer the surroundings; by the time we reached Lansdowne, at 6,000 feet, we were in good spirits.

The small hill station was a recruiting centre for the Garhwal Rifles (and still is), and did not cater to tourists. There were no hotels, just a couple of tea-stalls where a meal of dal and rice could be obtained. I believe it is much the same forty years on. Pratap had a friend who was the caretaker of an old, little used church, and he bedded us down in the vestry. Early next morning we set out on our long walk to Pratap's village.

I have covered longer distances on foot, but not all in one day. Thirty miles of trudging up hill and down and up again, most of it along a footpath that traversed bare hillsides where the hot May sun beat down relentlessly. Here and there we found a little shade and a freshet of spring water, which kept us going; but we had neglected to bring food with us apart from a couple of rock-hard buns probably dating back to colonial times, which we had picked up in Lansdowne. We were lucky to meet a farmer who gave us some onions and accompanied us part of the way.

Onions for lunch? Nothing better when you're famished. In the West they say, 'Never talk to strangers.' In the East they say, 'Always talk to strangers.' It was this stranger who gave us sustenance on the road, just as strangers had given me company on the way to the Pindar Glacier. On the open road there are no strangers. You share the same sky, the same mountain, the same sunshine and shade. On the open road we are all brothers.

The stranger went his way, and we went ours. 'Just a few more bends,' according to Pratap, always encouraging to the novice plainsman. But I was to be a hillman by the time we returned to Dehra! Hundreds of 'just a few more bends', before we reached the village, and I kept myself going with my off-key rendering of the old Harry Lauder song—

Keep right on to the end of the road,
Keep right on to the end.
If your way be long, let your heart be strong,
So keep right on round the bend.

By the time we'd done the last bend, I had a good idea of how the expression 'going round the bend' had came into existence. A maddened climber, such as I, had to negotiate one bend too many...

But Pratap was the right sort of companion. He adjusted his pace to suit mine; never lost patience; kept telling me I was a great walker. We arrived at the village just as night fell, and there was his mother waiting for us with a tumbler of milk.

Milk! I'd always hated the stuff (and still do) but that day I was grateful for it and drank two glasses. Fortunately it was cold. There was plenty of milk for me to drink during my two- week stay in the village, as Pratap's family possessed at least three productive cows. The milk was supplemented by thick rotis, made from grounded maize, seasonal vegetables, rice and a species of lentil peculiar to the area and very difficult to digest. Health-food friends would have approved of this fare, but it did not agree with me, and I found myself constipated most of the time. Still, better to be constipated than to be in free flow.

The point I am making is that it is always wise to carry your own food on a long hike or treks in the hills. Not that I could have done so, as Pratap's guest; he would have taken it as an insult. By the time I got back to Dehra—after another exhausted trek, and more complicated bus and train journeys—I felt quite famished and out of sorts. I bought some eggs and bacon rashers from the grocery store across the road from Astley Hall, and made myself a scrumptious breakfast. I am not much of a cook, but I can fry an egg and get the bacon nice and crisp. My needs are simple really. To each his own!

On another trek, from Mussoorie to Chamba (before the motor-road came into existence) I put two tins of sardines into my knapsack but forgot to take along a can-opener. Three days later I was back in Dehra, looking very thin indeed, and with my sardine tins still intact. That night I ate the contents of both tins.

Reading an account of the same trek undertaken by John Lang about a hundred years earlier, I was awestruck by his description of the supplies that he and his friends took with them.

Here he is, writing in Charles Dickens' magazine, *Household*

Words, in the issue of 30 January 1858:

> In front of the club-house our marching establishment
> had collected, and the one hundred and fifty coolies were
> laden with the baggage and stores. There were tents, camp
> tables, chairs, beds, bedding, boxes of every kind, dozens
> of cases of wine-port, sherry and claret-beer, ducks, fowls,
> geese, guns, umbrellas, great coats and the like.

He then goes on to talk of lobsters, oysters and preserved soups.

I doubt if I would have got very far on such fare. I took
the same road in October 1958, a century later; on my own
and without provisions except for the aforementioned sardine
tins. By dusk I had reached the village of Kaddukhal, where
the local shopkeeper put me up for the night.

I slept on the floor, on a sheepskin infested by fleas. They
were all over me as soon as I lay down, and I found it impossible
to sleep. I fled the shop before dawn.

'Don't go out before daylight,' warned my host. 'There are
bears around.'

But I would sooner have faced a bear than that onslaught
from the denizens of the sheepskin. And I reached Chamba in
time for an early morning cup of tea.

◆

Most Himalayan villages lie in the valleys, where there are small
streams, some farmland and protection from the biting winds
that come through the mountain passes. The houses are usually
made of large stones, and have sloping slate roofs so the heavy
monsoon rain can run off easily. During the sunny autumn
months, the roofs are often covered with pumpkins, left there
to ripen in the sun.

One October night, when I was sleeping at a friend's house just off the Tehri road, I was awakened by a rumbling and thumping on the roof. I woke my friend Jai and asked him what was happening.

'It's only a bear,' he said.

'Is it trying to get in?'

'No. It's after the pumpkins.'

A little later, when we looked out of a window, we saw a black bear making off through a field, leaving a trail of half-eaten pumpkins.

In winter, when snow covers the higher ranges, the Himalayan bears descend to lower altitudes in search of food. Sometimes they forage in fields. And because they are shortsighted and suspicious of anything that moves, they can be dangerous. But, like most wild animals, they avoid humans as much as possible.

Village folk always advise me to run downhill if chased by a bear. They say bears find it easier to run uphill than down. I have yet to be chased by a bear, and will happily skip the experience. But I have seen a few of these mountain bears and they are always fascinating to watch.

Himalayan bears enjoy corn, pumpkins, plums and apricots. Once, while I was sitting in an oak tree on Pari Tibba, hoping to see a pair of pine-martens that lived nearby, I heard the whining grumble of a bear, and presently a small bear ambled into the clearing beneath the tree.

He was little more than a cub, and I was not alarmed. I sat very still, waiting to see what the bear would do.

He put his nose to the ground and sniffed his way along until he came to a large anthill. Here he began huffing and puffing, blowing rapidly in and out of his nostrils so that the dust from the anthill flew in all directions. But the anthill had been deserted, and so, grumbling, the bear made his way up a nearby plum tree. Soon he was perched high in the branches. It was then that he saw me.

The bear at once scrambled several feet higher up the tree and lay flat on a branch. Since it wasn't a very big branch, there was a lot of bear showing on either side. He tucked his head behind another branch. He could no longer see me, so he apparently was satisfied that he was hidden, although he couldn't help grumbling.

Like all bears, this one was full of curiosity. So, slowly, inch by inch, his black snout appeared over the edge of the branch. As soon as he saw me, he drew his head back and hid his face.

He did this several times. I waited until he wasn't looking, then moved some way down my tree. When the bear looked over and saw that I was missing, he was so pleased that he stretched right across to another branch and helped himself to a plum. At that, I couldn't help bursting into laughter.

The startled young bear tumbled out of the tree, dropped through the branches some fifteen feet, and landed with a thump in a pile of dried leaves. He was unhurt, but fled from the clearing, grunting and squealing all the way.

Another time, my friend Jai told me that a bear had been active in his cornfield. We took up a post at night in an old cattle shed, which gave a clear view of the moonlit field.

A little after midnight, the bear came down to the edge of the field. She seemed to sense that we had been about. She was hungry, however. So, after standing on her hind legs and peering around to make sure the field was empty, she came cautiously out of the forest.

The bear's attention was soon distracted by some Tibetan prayer flags, which had been strung between two trees. She gave a grunt of disapproval and began to back away, but the fluttering of the flags was a puzzle that she wanted to solve. So she stopped and watched them.

Soon the bear advanced to within a few feet of the flags, examining them from various angles. Then, seeing that they posed no danger, she went right up to the flags and pulled them down. Grunting with apparent satisfaction, she moved into the field of corn.

Jai had decided that he didn't want to lose any more of his crop, so he started shouting. His children woke up and soon came running from the house, banging on empty kerosene tins.

Deprived of her dinner, the bear made off in a bad temper. She ran downhill at a good speed, and I was glad that I was not in her way.

Uphill or downhill, an angry bear is best given a very wide path.

♦

Sleeping out, under the stars, is a very romantic conception. 'Stones thy pillow, earth thy bed,' goes an old hymn, but a rolled-up towel or shirt will make a more comfortable pillow Do not settle down to sleep on sloping ground, as I did once when I was a Boy Scout during my prep school days. We had camped at Tara Devi, on the outskirts of Shimla, and as it was a warm night I decided to sleep outside our tent. In the middle of the night I began to roll. Once you start rolling on a steep hillside, you don't stop. Had it not been for a thorny dog-rose bush, which halted my descent, I might well have rolled over the edge of a precipice.

I had a wonderful night once, sleeping on the sand on the banks of the Ganga above Rishikesh. It was a balmy night, with just a faint breeze blowing across the river, and as I lay there looking up at the stars, the lines of a poem by R.L. Stevenson kept running through my head:

> Give to me the life I love,
> Let the lave go by me,
> Give the jolly heaven above
> And the byway nigh me.
> Bed in the bush with stars to see,
> Bread I dip in the river—
> There's the life for a man like me,
> There's the life for ever.

The following night I tried to repeat the experience, but the jolly heaven above opened up in the early hours, the rain came pelting down, and I had to run for shelter to the nearest Ashram. Never take Mother Nature for granted!

The best kind of walk, and this applies to the plains as well as to the hills, is the one in which you have no particular destination when you set out.

'Where are you off?' asked a friend of mine the other day, when he met me on the road.

'Honestly, I have no idea,' I said, and I was telling the truth.

I did end up in Happy Valley, where I met an old friend whom I hadn't seen for years. When we were boys, his mother used to tell us stories about the bhoots that haunted her village near Mathura. We reminisced and then went our different ways. I took the road to Hathipaon and met a schoolgirl who covered ten miles every day on her way to and from her school. So there were still people who used their legs, though out of necessity rather than choice.

Anyway, she gave me a story to write and thus I ended the

day with two stories, one a memoir and the other based on a fresh encounter. And all because I had set out without a plan. The adventure is not in getting somewhere, it's the on-the-way experience. It is not the expected; it's the surprise. Not the fulfilment of prophecy, but the providence of something better than that prophesied.